Jame

# BEHIND
## THE
# TWISTED
# FENCE

Paperback ISBN 978-0-6483793-0-0

Dear Ember, Ryder and Mel,
Where would I be without you?

# Preface

When a tale is told enough times, it tends to change. Sometimes the storyteller omits things to make the tale simpler or shorter. Other times, stories are changed to hide the truth.

The tale of Jack and the Beanstalk is one such story and the truth starts with the magic that created those beans. After the beanstalk incident, some powerful people decided that magic was far too dangerous for anyone to use, especially for children. But children are curious and none more so than a girl called Zelie. It's ten years since Jack chopped down the beanstalk and Zelie has spent her whole life surrounded by rules she doesn't understand. She knows it's not allowed, but magic is just too exciting to resist. It couldn't be as dangerous as they say.

Or could it?

# CHAPTER ONE

## *The Fence*

Zelie's misty breaths escaped her trembling lips and dissolved, one after another, into the gloom. For the third time this week she was standing in Mahogany Lane, absently pinching at the calluses on her hands, jiggling her knees back and forth to keep warm. All the while, she gazed silently at the twisted fence. It was a tall crooked structure held together by barbed wire and black tar, and packed so densely with gnarled branches that it was impossible to see through. It looked as if it should have fallen down long ago. But according to the stories, it had stood for many years. And for just about that long, everyone on the island had avoided anything to do with it. The adults would not even talk about it with Zelie.

"Hush now, child," they would say. "Commit your mind to questions with happier answers."

Nothing would stop the kids from making up stories though. There were all kinds of rumours about this place whispered inside cupped hands. Zelie had heard many tales. And while she had long since given up the belief in a mysterious witch and an ugly screeching ghoul who could freeze anyone who entered, other stories were quite convincing. All of them involved horrible torture, slavery or imprisonment as penalty for disturbing the variously described resident on the other side of this fence. Apparently, her father had met his demise here before the fence was even built. But she was not permitted to know anything more. Over the years, her curiosity had become even stronger than her fear for this place. Yet she knew to be careful. There was no sense in disturbing the silence in case any of the stories *were* true.

She picked out two paths she could take to the top of the fence where she could avoid slipping on moss or being scratched by jagged branches or barbed wire. But, as usual, a dull tint was creeping like a slow infection across the low sky. There was little time before nightfall and now that clammy sense of fear was threatening to take over again.

With a shake of her head, she pushed everything but the fence from her mind and stepped forward carefully. She gripped a rusted fence pole with one hand and a curled branch with the other and gently lifted her foot off the gravel path.

The fence leaned towards her and groaned, stabbing the silence. She stepped back and raised her hands in case the fence was about to fall on her. But it had tilted as far as it was going to and now towered over her like a cruel teenager, daring her to try again. Her body trembled like electrified steel and her heart rattled noisily in her chest.

It was not just the thought of being crushed by the fence but the vague threat of being heard by whatever evil lay on the other side that gave her worry. But, to her relief, she heard no reply to her noisy blunder. She took another minute to compose herself and then began to climb.

Loose twigs on the fence protested her ascent. They clawed at her clothes and scratched her skin as she rose around and through the curls and loops of creaking branches and squeaking wire. Her fingers were cold but her arms warmed quickly from the effort.

Her first glimpse over the fence was a blur; a quick scan for danger or movement on the other side. Then, shaking from the effort of climbing, she heaved her body on top of the fence.

Gazing through the haze of exertion, her eyes came into focus on the garden on the other side. A giddy warmth spread through Zelie's body. She had finally done it. This was the only part of the tiny island she had never seen. She had imagined that the space inside the fence would look much like the outside—mean, unkempt, and full of hate, but the garden below her was nothing like that.

To one side of a clearing was a house made of stone. Smoke floated from the chimney in wisps and vanished into the darkening sky. On the far side of the clearing stood a wooden stable and a few wobbly looking structures with battered tin roofs. Beyond those there was a cliff where the land dropped away to the dark and restless sea below. Zelie could see now that the twisted fence ran from the edge of the cliff, around the house and gardens and back to the cliff edge. There was only one large gate to provide entrance but from the heavy chains and padlocks that secured it closed, Zelie deduced that it was seldom used.

At the base of the fence, the dense pale grass was cropped carpet short and bordered by a low crimson hedge trimmed perfectly square. Three tiny garden gnomes, set in comical poses, were arranged in a group at the base of the fence. Next to them, a large collection of brown soggy leaves had been raked neatly into an impossibly tall round heap.

Zelie's initial feeling of elation gave way to a strange disappointment. There was no hint of hostility or danger. There was little adventure here: no answers to be found or anything to tell her friends. Whoever lived on the other side of the fence appeared to live a neat and eventless life. Perhaps the rumours were simply schoolyard stories made up by bored older kids to scare the younger ones.

She had once thought her mother dodged or ignored questions about her father because she wanted to protect Zelie from some horror or to avoid reliving the painful memory of his loss, so she never pressed for answers. But now she felt frustrated at the needless secrecy.

Don't be silly, she told herself. If anything, she should be grateful to have somewhere new to climb and explore.

As Zelie's gaze shifted back to the pile of leaves at the base of the fence, a wave of excitement washed away all other thoughts. The climb had not been for nothing. Though it was becoming dark, a big squashy pile of leaves at the base of a fence was not an opportunity she was going to pass up.

With a broad smile, she shuffled along the top rail of the fence, now free of care for the creaks and groans it emitted. Then, careful to keep her balance, she stood up in readiness to leap.

The fence squeaked as Zelie launched herself into the air. The wind whooshed past. It lifted her hair and fluttered her dress until she landed with a squelch, dislodging a clump of leaves which rolled down the side of the pile to the ground and knocked over one of the garden gnomes with a *clink*. Zelie peeled the cold sticky leaves from her giggling face.

A door squeaked open inside the house and a light flickered on. Then came a harsh mechanical squeal which pulled Zelie's face into a grimace. It took her a moment to realise it was a human voice, though she had never heard a person, nor even the most abused of farming equipment, make a more disagreeable noise. Could the rumour about the ghoul be true after all? Zelie shuffled to the base of the pile and swept some leaves over her so that she could not be seen. Then she peered out, curious to see what kind of creature could produce such a blaring unbearable sound.

A dark figure appeared in the window, thrashing and dancing to the angry tune of the screeching voice. It was not a ghoul but a tattered old woman. The words were too muffled to understand, but the tone was clear: such hostility, such untamed fury. The window rattled abruptly open.

"You must have the mind of a trout," screeched the voice, which was now agonisingly clear without the closed window to dampen it. It rasped and grated in Zelie's ears like a rusty wheel and sent an aching itch all the way down her spine. Wincing, Zelie clamped her hands tightly over her ears but the words cut right through. "This cabbage soup has more intelligence than you Sawyer, you great baboon! Magic beans. Pah! There's no magic in these!" A hand flashed into view, casting a small object into the air which then bounced and rolled onto the illuminated patch of grass in the clearing.

"No!" cried a boy's desperate voice.

"And you swapped my favourite cow for them, Sawyer, you imbecile! They're not worth a bag of horse manure. Besides that, magic's illegal or had that slipped out of your tiny brain."

"Please Auntie, I need them. If I could just go outside and-"

"No you cannot, Sawyer. Now get to bed. And no soup. Go on. Get."

Bang went the window. The glass rattled and the voice muffled and screeched on without pause.

Zelie stayed still. Whoever made up those schoolyard stories was doing kids a favour. It might not be a ghoul that lived here but it sounded like one. Perhaps it was the villagers that built the fence in the first place. No good could come from being anywhere near this house. For a moment, Zelie thought of the boy. What was his name? She tried to replay the argument in her head, but instead of the boy's name, Zelie remembered something else. The boy called her 'Auntie' didn't he? And hadn't he stolen a cow? Well then, maybe he deserved exactly what he was getting. In any case, it was none of her business and there was nothing here that she cared to experience again. It might be better to leave quietly and forget all about this place.

She could not simply get up and climb the fence now. No way. If that lady opened the window again, Zelie would be spotted for sure. But how could she tolerate the torture of this voice until she made her escape?

You'll just have to put up with it, she told herself, resolving to stay hidden as long as it took for the lights to go off. She stuck a finger deep in each ear and waited.

In that moment, Zelie felt a silly sense of pride knowing that none of her friends would have this problem: hidden in a pile of leaves in a mysterious garden. On first glance, Zelie looked like any other twelve-year-old girl in town, though her face was thinner—probably because she missed so many meals. Despite that, she was stronger than most of the boys from all the climbing she did. Her mother would call her blond plait 'straggly' but it did not worry her, nor did she care that her clothes were often covered with dirt or bark from some earlier adventure.

With her fingers buried in her ears, she gazed up at the cloud that blanketed the island village of Emerson. It was growing dark. Somewhere above the cloud the sun must have been setting—at least that was what she had been told. She had lived most of her life under a cursed sky and had no memory of the sun. The depth of grey in the cloud was the only thing that ever distinguished night from day and, now, it was almost black.

Zelie had a faint notion of a bright blue sky that radiated warmth. But was it a memory or, rather, her imagination after all the stories she had heard? Her mother's close friend, Jack, spoke a lot about what it was like before 'the curse'. He talked about the sun the way her mother used to tell a fairy tale. And that was how Zelie always thought of it: magical and entertaining, but not real. She never really understood why everyone's longing seemed so deep. To Zelie, the thought of the sun—a burning ball of gas in the sky— just seemed bizarre. She believed it existed, in the same way she believed that the world was actually round, even though the endless ocean that surrounded their tiny island suggested the planet was flat. But grey sky and pale light never prevented her from doing anything she wanted. So why should she worry?

The voice squawked a little louder and Zelie thought for a moment the woman might be coming outside. She shuffled deeper into the leaf pile and wriggled until enough leaves fell over her that she was completely hidden. Her back was pressing up against something hard which smelled wet and rotten and she tried her best not to think what it could be.

After a while, she forgot about the smell. The space beneath the leaves began to warm up. But the voice never stopped. How much longer could this woman possibly complain?

Zelie closed her eyes and tried to make a game of her situation, picking out all the horrible elements that made up the lady's screech: a high-pitched squeak like a broken tractor, a grinding sound like rocks being ground to dust, and a buzzing hum like a speaker turned up way too loud. Then she let those sounds drift back together until it became a drone that went on and on and on…

# CHAPTER TWO

## *Inside the Garden*

Zelie awoke with a gentle twitch, yawned and stretched her arms and legs like a cat. Wet leaves fell all around her. *Leaves?*

How could she have possibly fallen asleep with that lady's grinding voice in her ears?

Night had long since fallen. In fact, for a moment, Zelie thought it might be daybreak. There was a faint glimmer of light peeking through Zelie's leafy camouflage. But it was not like the dull haze she knew to be the usual foggy colour of day. This light was sort of… cheerful.

That was Jack's word. "It's the way you feel when you see a sunset or a rainbow," he said, as if that meant anything to Zelie. "Like the fluttering of a hundred butterflies in your belly," he added. As if that made it clearer. What was a butterfly, anyway?

Curious about the source of the 'cheerful' glow, Zelie pushed a swathe of leaves aside and twisted her fists in her eye sockets to rub away sleep's glaze. The window of the house was dark now, and all was silent, thank goodness. The glow was coming from something lying on the grass. Squinting, Zelie could just make out a crumpled paper bag. A gentle blue light pulsed, like a calm heart beat, through the bag's creases and out through its loosely twisted opening. This must have been what the lady threw out the window and what the boy so desperately wanted.

The leaves peeled off Zelie's clothes as she crawled, wide-eyed, from her warm enclosure into the damp night air towards this strange specimen. Reaching out with one hand, she unraveled the bag end.

Blinding bright light streamed out of the opening of the paper bag, stinging her eyes. It was so bright that even after turning away, she could still see the outline of the bag's opening. It was as if the shape had been imprinted on her eyes. She blinked until it began to dim. Still with her back to the light, her eyes came into focus on one of the dusty garden gnomes illuminated in the beam of bright light. It was the red gnome that she knocked over as she landed on the leaf pile. Its rosy face was tilted slightly upwards at the two standing beside it and there was a large fresh hole in side of its face.

Zelie turned back to the glowing paper bag. Squinting through one eye, she scooped it up and shook it out. Four short curved beans rolled into her cupped hand. At the instant the beans touched her skin, a soothing warmth spread through the palm of her hand and up her arm. But this was warmth unlike any other; not even the comfort of defrosting her hands on a warm cup of her mother's potato stew could compare to this. It was like the heat was rising from within her. In that moment, it felt as if she would never be cold again.

The beans were decorated with delicate swirls and curls, which linked and flowed together as if they had been painted in luminous ink by a careful hand. The light seemed to pulse from inside the beans through their patterned skin. She closed her hand around them and admired the gentle light shining through the gaps in her fingers. How long she stared, trance-like into their beautiful light, Zelie did not know. But the shock that followed almost stopped her heart as the screeching voice cut through the silence.

"SAWYER, you rodent! You left the light on outside again!"

The air was suddenly icy, and Zelie puffed out a cloud of mist as she jumped to her feet, fumbled the beans into the paper bag and crammed them in a pocket. The next moment, she was running, leaping over the gnomes and onto the fence. Behind her, a door squeaked open.

"…pitiful excuse for a boy. I'll send you to the witch for her experiments if you keep on…" The squawking stopped at its loudest. And then…

"Who is that? How the devil? What are you doing in here?"

But Zelie did not answer or even turn her head to see. She just climbed. The warmth of the beans had evaporated and her fingers felt like icicles. Frost appeared on the sleeves of her jacket—just like the rumours. Up and through the tangle of branches she weaved. Twigs pulled at her even more insistently than before. They snapped off in her hair and clothes. Zelie could hear the heavy clomping of angry footsteps approaching from behind.

With a thud, a broom speared into the fence, just inches from her ribs.

"Missed. Blast!" The voice felt like a fork being twisted inside Zelie's head. "Get out of my garden you nasty little insect. Out!"

Zelie climbed faster, bracing her body against whatever else the lady happened to throw at her. The screeching voice was beneath her now.

"Yes, hurry little cockroach. Scurry away quickly before I squash you into mush with my boot."

In a neat movement, Zelie hooked her aching fingers on the ridge of the fence, flicked her body over the top, hopped off the terrace wall, and landed with a barely audible crunch on the gravel. Her heart thumped at her ribs and an unlikely smile crept onto her face. An Olympic gymnast would struggle to dismount with that sort of finesse. She folded her frosty arms tightly across her chest and, filled with jaunty pride, jogged off down the alley.

"Goodies!" the lady shrieked through the fence, her voice laden with malicious delight. Zelie had to stifle a laugh. "Mmm. Yes, sweet goodies, I'm sure," her voice squeaked, almost inquisitively. "Leave out something sweet, bugs on your feet. Put those sweets away, bugs won't come today." The voice wailed, like a broken violin. "Well you had your chance, Insect." On the other side of the fence, Zelie could hear a series of thuds as the lady pounded and stomped at the earth.

Pressing her hands over her ears, Zelie shook her head at the lady's madness.

"That will teach you, you vile cockroach," said the rattling voice. "That's what happens to anything that comes in here, including you if you come back. Now get lost. Go on, get!"

Zelie thought this was probably the only bit of sense the lady had spoken. So she jogged away through the dark lane towards the streetlights. A gentle breeze ushered away the icy chill and returned a familiar dampness. As the frost began to melt on her jacket, she slowed to a walk, still breathing heavily, and tried to cobble some meaning out of the lady's shrieking babble. A quick check over her shoulder told her she was safely alone but at that very moment, a flash shone from behind the fence.

Zelie frowned as two more bright beams lit up the night sky like camera flashes. Perhaps the lady was taking photographs. At nighttime? She did seem crazy enough to do something like that.

Since she was a safe distance away, Zelie decided to venture another peak at the beans. Standing under a streetlight, she reached inside her pocket, barely able to wait for her numb fingers to retrieve her warm treasure.

Zelie knew something was wrong the moment she touched it. The bag was crumpled and limp. As she tipped it, a single bean rolled out of a tattered hole into Zelie's hand. The bean was cold and dull and she could see none of the patterns that had mesmerised her earlier.

She closed her eyes tight and scowled at the sky as the realisation sunk in. In her haste to put the bag away, it had torn open. Three of the beans must have fallen out somewhere in the garden. The angry lady was talking about 'goodies'. Now Zelie guessed that she had been cursing and stomping on those beautiful beans. And to make things worse, this remaining one had lost its glow and warmth.

Zelie groaned. She was tired, confused and upset. Carefully buttoning the last bean in her pocket, she hurried on her way.

Though she had no clue what time it was, she had a strange urge to knock on Jack's door as she passed by his house. She could not ask him directly about magic. He just would not have it. But if she asked enough questions, he would often talk enough to let something slip. It was from Jack that she learned most of what she knew about her father. The rest she learned from listening carefully to adults when they thought she could not hear.

Apparently, her father had been the Mayor of Emerson and a great supporter of magic. Then 'the curse' happened and he died. Though Zelie did not know the details, she was certain there was a magical element to both events. That was probably why his replacement, Mayor Andrews, was so opposed to spells of any kind. In fact, as well as being illegal, the mere mention of magic had ladies clutching their chests and men muttering nervously.

Perhaps if she got Jack talking, she could learn more about the magic beans. She walked up the path towards Jack's front door. There was a large dark shape sitting on his front lawn and while Zelie was trying to determine what it was, she tripped over some sort of heavy cable and bumped her elbow on the ground.

A light came on inside Jack's house and the sounds of movement could be heard. But Zelie was too embarrassed to stay now. She could not have Jack knowing that she had tripped over on flat ground. What would he think of her? Ignoring the pain, she hurried to her feet, hurdled the cable, pushed through the gate and ran all the way home.

# CHAPTER THREE

## *Waking up at home*

Beth's warm arms closed around Zelie's body and squeezed her awake in bed.

"You're home. My darling, thank goodness, you're safe."

"Hi Mum," Zelie croaked. Her bleary morning gaze came into focus on her bookshelf which was lined with gifts that Beth had given her in various attempts to nurture less dangerous passions. She had cookbooks, a jewellery-making kit, a chess board, and a range of other items intended to promote quiet activities. Every one of them had been gathering dust for over a year. Zelie would have preferred a new pair of boots. But, she never asked, fearing it might cause an argument.

She huffed as Beth's squeeze tightened and awoke the graze on her elbow.

"I do get worried when you come home so late," said Beth. "What's this? You're still in your clothes."

"It was dark, Mum. I might have woken you up if I tried to find my pajamas," Zelie said, arching her back and stretching her legs and arms out.

"I wouldn't have minded. Oh my, just look at the state of you," Beth said, chuckling, as she picked small sticks and half-dried bits of leaves out of the tangles of Zelie's hair. "Where have you been this time?"

Beth would occasionally ask about Zelie's adventures because there was little else that Zelie spoke about with any passion. But then Beth would become upset when Zelie mentioned anything that sounded dangerous. To Beth, most of what Zelie did was dangerous so Zelie was constantly trying to avoid giving too much detail.

"I went exploring through one of the gardens in the village," began Zelie. "I climbed up really high and then I jumped into this big pile of leaves. It was so good." Zelie was becoming more awake and animated as the memories flowed back.

"Oh, that's lovely," said Beth in the same voice she used after finding out her Christmas present from Jack last year was a bike helmet. The last time Beth rode a bike she was in primary school.

"And I found this strange bean," continued Zelie. "Here, it's still in my pocket. Look."

"A bean?" replied Beth, her voice changing tone as she took the bean to inspect it. "What makes you think it's strange?"

Had she said too much already? "Maybe it's not that strange. I don't know much about beans, I guess."

Zelie looked up at Beth, whose interest had dissolved into a sort of confusion.

"Can I have it back?"

If anything Beth looked more worried as she slowly placed the bean back in Zelie's hand and closed it with a gentle squeeze. With an angled stare Beth left the room without saying another word.

*

While she was eating breakfast, Zelie had been massaging the bean in her free hand, trying to bring it back to life. Surely somehow she could reignite its glow and warmth? But nothing seemed to be working.

After breakfast, Beth's spirits seemed to have been restored and she offered to wash Zelie's hair. It was particularly filthy after last night so Zelie agreed without her usual fuss.

Reluctantly, she placed the bean at the very back of a shelf on the wall of the bathroom. Then she sat down and tilted her head backwards into a basin which Beth had filled with warm water.

"Just look at all these split ends," said Beth. "If you would look after your hair, I expect it would grow a little longer."

Beth loved the story of Rapunzel: the princess who let down her golden hair. In fact, that's where the name 'Zelie' came from. But no matter how many times Beth told her that story, Zelie could not seem to care what her hair looked like. What was the point?

"I swear, I should have named you Goldilocks," Beth said as she lathered shampoo into Zelie's dirty blond mop. This was a joke that Beth made quite often. Usually, Beth would continue by suggesting it was lucky Zelie disliked porridge, otherwise one of her adventures might have found her disagreeing with a family of bears over food and furniture. But today, she stopped short.

"So, tell me more about this adventure of yours," said Beth, as she tugged the comb through a painful tangle.

This was unusual. Zelie could not remember the last time Beth asked her twice about any of her exploits. What more could Zelie say that would not upset her?

It would be safest to talk about escaping the garden. She had been shooed out of more than half of the gardens in the village and, because she tended to make quite a mess, she had been called every name under the sun in the process. Beth was quite used to hearing about it. So Zelie was quite surprised at the severity of Beth's reaction. As Zelie said the word 'insect', Beth's breath caught in her throat and she lurched backwards as if she had been struck on the forehead. Zelie heard a wooden bump as Beth hit the bathroom shelf hard. Among the sounds of bottles falling onto the floor, there was a metallic ting and Zelie opened her eyes to see a small dull lump falling from the direction of the ceiling towards her. Beth gave a wheezy gasp, shuffled her feet in desperation and reached out a hand to catch it but missed.

Plop, went the lump as it fell in the basin.

A bright flash lit up the room and a jolt ran through Zelie's scalp. Then all the lights in the house went out at once. Zelie shrieked and stood up.

"What was that?" she said, as water sloshed down her back onto the chair and floor. Beth made a movement towards the basin; then she hesitated.

"The bean fell in," Beth said. There was regret and fear in her voice.

"What? No!" shrieked Zelie, plunging her hands through the foam.

Beth gasped and put a hand over her mouth as if Zelie had just put her hands into a fire.

"I can't find it." Zelie shrieked.

"Dear oh dear," muttered Beth as Zelie searched blindly under the bubbles over every square inch of the basin until all the foam had disappeared.

"That was the last one," Zelie said, miserably, plopping down on the wet chair, not caring about the water seeping through her pajamas. Shoulders slumped, hands in her lap, hair dripping, she stared ahead. Even when the lights came back on, neither of them reacted.

After a minute, Beth sighed and reached for a towel. "I had better dry your hair," she said, listlessly. "I don't want you to catch a cold."

Zelie shrugged. She realised now that it was not just the warmth of the beans or their luminous swirls that held her interest. They held the promise of discovery and germinated within her a feeling of connection with her father. If he had believed in magic, there must have been a good reason. Now, she would never know.

Beth was clearly deep in thought as well. As she rubbed Zelie's hair dry, she began to mutter. Most of what Beth was saying was a mumble but the words that Zelie could hear were enough to restore a tiny ray of hope.

"…know it was *that* kind of bean… activated by the… an improvement, usually…"

She was rubbing the same patch of Zelie's head over and over even though it was dry and the rest of her hair was still dripping.

"I could have sworn… a concoction? —no, surely not."

Zelie would rarely ask any questions about such ramblings. But now the beans were gone, she felt frustrated and reckless.

"Mum?"

Beth did not answer. Zelie lifted the towel and peered up at her vacant eyes. She was as still as a picture, brow furrowed, eyes locked onto the water in the basin, as if in a trance.

"Mum," repeated Zelie.

"Hmm?" said Beth, seeming mildly irritated at the intrusion.

"What's a concoction?"

Beth's gaze met Zelie's. Her eyes widened and jittered in their sockets as if searching for something around Zelie's head. "It's Tuesday isn't it?" she said suddenly as if she had found what she was looking for. "Music lesson today. You had better get moving," she said, lifting Zelie off the chair and ushering her away from the basin still with the towel over her head.

"It's Friday," Zelie said, trying not to slip over on the

wet floor.

"Well, there's no harm in arriving at school a little early is there?"

Zelie bumped her sore elbow on the doorframe. "Ow! Mum, stop pushing!"

"It was strange that the lights went out, wasn't it?" Beth continued, bustling Zelie onwards to her bedroom. "I'd say there's a loose wire somewhere. I'll have to ask Jack to check it."

"Mum!"

Beth gave one more shove that sent Zelie inside the doorway of her room. "There you are, Dear. Now, you get ready quickly while I go make you something nice for lunch. Maybe a little treat too? I'm sure I have a little chocolate hidden away from Easter." And with that, Beth shot up the hallway to the kitchen.

Zelie rubbed her elbow. Treats for lunch? That never happened. And loose wiring? What was she on about?

Whatever caused that flash and the blackout did seem electrical though. Almost like the camera flashes that shone up from behind the fence last night.

The beans in the garden, of course! It was exactly the same kind of flash. No, but they can't have disappeared, she tried to tell herself. It wasn't that wet on the ground. Those flashes must have been something else. The beans are still there. And when I go back there after school, I'm going to find them.

"Are you ready?" Beth called out. "Come on, I'll drive you to school."

# CHAPTER FOUR

## *Returning to the Garden*

Zelie galloped up to her house, thrust the key into the lock and crashed through the door. Her hands were a blur as she unpacked her bag, changed into trousers, a shirt and a thick sweater, and grabbed Beth's garden trowel off the hook in the garage. She was halfway down the street when she remembered she had not locked the door and had to turn back.

Surely there was a chance that at least one bean was still lying at the base of the fence, relatively unharmed? Yes, that angry lady stomped her selfish boots all over them but they must be able to withstand a little battering. There had been no rain during the day to dissolve them, but it would not be long before the next downpour. It never was. Zelie was racing against nature itself.

When she closed her eyes, the bean's intricate swirls and hypnotic glow were so clear in her mind that she could almost see them on the back of her eyelids. But the comfort of their warmth was like a half-remembered dream. A surge of excitement ran through her at the thought of holding them in her hand again and her pace quickened.

The afternoon sky was a disinterested grey over a restless sea. The cold and rusty play equipment begged her for one swing, one slide, one anything. But she ignored them all. Before the curse, people used to come down here to the seaside in tiny clothes that left their arms and legs completely bare. Shorts and t-shirts, they were called. Zelie wore more than that for underwear. Jack said they would flock here wearing these little strips of clothing and get into that grey water, for fun. But nobody even thought of doing that now.

In fact, Zelie created quite a stir last week when she fell into the cold sea. Some children had braved the drizzle to kick around a ball in the park. Zelie was passing by on her way back from Jack's house when the ball was accidentally kicked off the bank into the water. It had drifted under the old dead tree that leaned out over the water. Zelie had always thought that the tree's bent shape made it appear as if it were trying to flee the village. She knew how it felt. Though she was quite afraid of falling in, she climbed that old tree and dangled upside down to rescue the ball. But the old branches were too weak to hold her. When they broke, she fell head-first into the freezing water. None of the children in the village could swim, including Zelie. It was always far too cold to learn how. But somehow, she paddled out of that freezing salty water alive. She even retrieved the ball. It took more than two hours under a warm shower to get sensation back in her toes.

If not for the newly built terrace of houses on the other side of the park, she would have been able to walk directly up the hill to Mahogany Lane. As it was, she had to make her way though the outskirts of the village past Jack's house.

Jack was in his front garden chopping with an axe and breathing heavily as Zelie approached. His brown hair was damp with sweat and steam was rising from the top of his head.

"Hey Jack," Zelie called as she jogged towards him.

Jack glanced her way and leaned on the handle of his axe, looking glad for an opportunity to rest. He wiped the sweat from his dark eyebrows with the back of his hand, and smiled.

"There you are, Squirrel. It's been donkey's years." He was full of funny old phrases even though Zelie guessed he could not be much older than twenty. 'Squirrel' was a nickname that he had given her a few years ago because, he said, she was always climbing trees and chasing some nutty idea.

"You're just in time. Take a gander at the size of this thing," Jack said, tapping his axe on the side of an enormous pumpkin as round as a tractor tyre and as high as his waist. "This one pumpkin will make enough soup for the next two market days."

This was the dark object she had seen last night in his garden. Connected to it, and lying across the path, was the cable-like vine that she had tripped over though she was not about to let Jack know anything about that.

"Charmed seeds? Jack, you'll get in trouble," she whispered.

"What?" Jack said, feigning innocence. "It's not like I cast the spell myself. The seeds were already like that when I bought them."

"You could have planted it in your back garden where nobody would see."

"I did, Squirrel. It was hidden away nicely and my little secret was safe. But vines like to explore—especially charmed ones. And this little rascal found its way right round the side of the house into full view before it decided to fruit."

Zelie smiled. It was encouraging when Jack pushed the boundaries. Jack seemed to read her expression.

"Now Squirrel, don't you get any ideas about doing something like this yourself," warned Jack. "I might be able to get away with a small enchantment here and there, but it's still against the law."

Zelie nodded solemnly. A boy at her school was caught using magic once. He went to the village markets and swapped his best scarf for a small magic rhinestone. The lady that sold it said it he could wave it over any computer screen to jumble up the letters, making them spell out rude jokes or the answers on school tests, depending on which way he waved it. The boy had it hidden inside one of his gloves. But when he tried to use it in class, nothing happened. In a rage, he took the rhinestone out of his glove and jumped on it until it cracked and a green gooey substance began to spew out.

Zelie was doing a test in the classroom down the hall at the time. She heard a distant collective shriek and assumed there was some sort of science experiment going on. So she ignored the strong smell of old socks that arrived about a minute later but the squeak of skin on glass made her look up from her test. At least twenty children and their teacher were sliding down the hallway past her classroom window on a slow green wave of smelly jelly. Zelie's class had to climb out through the fire escape and school was cancelled for the rest of the week.

The boy was suspended for a whole year and the smell stayed for almost that long. The rumour was that the Mayor Andrews and his scientists locked the boy away for treatment of some kind. When he came back he was pale and as thin as a stick and he barely spoke above a whisper.

"Silly to have a law against magic isn't it?" said Jack. "I know we're not supposed to talk about it but that anti-magic law is the reason that all the trade ships stopped coming to our ports. It was nothing to do with the cloud like Mayor Andrews says. Still, I'm sure folk wouldn't stay here twiddling their freezing thumbs on this island if there were plenty of boats to escape on. Then who would eat me delicious pumpkin soup."

"Couldn't we just change the law?"

"There's the pickle, Squirrel. Even if people decided they didn't like the law, they're not allowed to talk about it. Ha," laughed Jack. "And here I am running me mouth at a hundred mile an hour on the very topic we're not supposed to discuss."

"I wish you could say more."

"Me too Squirrel. Me too. Things will change, eventually. They always do. Sadly, it's not going to happen today, so I better get this pumpkin out of sight before Mayor Andrews catches wind of it. Give me an hour or so and I'll have cleared enough space for your dizzy antics. Those cartwheels are really coming along."

"Actually, I won't today. There's somewhere else I have to go."

"Course there is, Squirrel. I see that curious look on your mug. Don't worry. I won't ask any questions. Well, off you trot then. And keep the sun in your heart." That was a saying that many of the adults used instead of 'good bye'. It made no sense to Zelie.

"See you later Jack. And good luck with that vine," she said.

"Don't want luck. I want lunch." Jack winked as he lifted the heavy axe over his shoulder. Zelie chuckled and turned. The echo of rhythmic chopping followed her down the street.

*

Zelie was literally bouncing by the time she turned down the back of the terrace onto Mahogany Lane. The gravel scuffed under her feet as she skipped along, humming a tune and twirling the trowel by the loop on its handle.

Suddenly, her breath seemed to freeze inside her

lungs and an arctic chill ran up her spine. She skidded to a halt at the very corner of the twisted fence. Ice crystals tinkled to the ground as the water froze out of the very air. Tiny shards of ice prickled inside her nose and throat. Even the gravel seemed to have frozen to the ground. Zelie knew this aching cold from last time she was in the garden but this time it seemed much more severe. An angry muttering broke the freezing silence.

The muttering grew louder and more painful as she tiptoed down the lane. The ice in her throat was unbearable. As silently as possible, she buried her mouth in the elbow fold of her jacket and coughed. Her nose was already numb and her ear lobes ached as if they might turn to ice, split away from her head and shatter like glass on the ground. And then there was the torturous voice which rattled her bones and made her grit her teeth so hard that they squeaked. The densely twisted wood of the towering fence seemed to do nothing to dampen it. But as repellent as it was, the pull of the beans and their mysteries was still greater.

The words faded into comprehension. Was she yelling at a tree?

"… aren't even proper branches. You think you're so special with your skinny, wobbly trunk and your silly leaves blocking what precious little light I can get through that cloud," she spat. "Where is that boy? Sawyer!" A brief silence was like a moment of weightlessness. Then the voice came again like a jackhammer and Zelie's skull felt as if it would split in two. "Come out here."

A door squeaked open somewhere behind the fence.

"Yes, Auntie Ruth?" came a frightened little voice.

"Look at this… *thing*. Look how it catches the eye. It is not neat. It is not pretty. What's it doing here?"

"I don't know Auntie," said the boy in a pleading voice.

"The garden is your responsibility. How could you not know?" shrieked the angry lady. "Pig! That's what you are. A filthy lying swine!"

"Auntie Ruth, please. Not again. Look. I'll chop it down right now."

"Give me that axe. Pig! You had your chance. Now, into the hog house. And take your toothbrush."

The boy sighed. "Can't I please use the hose to clean them this time?"

"Toothbrush, I said! Are you deaf? I want those pigs smelling as sweet as roses. Now get!"

A moment later, from the other side of the fence came a series of weak thuds, which Zelie took to be Auntie Ruth chopping at something.

Seeking some thread of sense, Zelie turned her curious gaze towards the sky and gasped. An enormous green plant stared down at her from the other side of the fence. The plant was as high as three houses stacked on top of one another. Its two thin green stems coiled around each other up into the grey sky like duelling pythons in a whirling embrace. Leaves as big as bath towels extended from the stems. Where had it come from? It was not there last night and nothing grew that big overnight. Someone must have planted it there. Not Sawyer, at least not on his own and not without a crane or a team of gardeners to lift it in place. But Auntie Ruth seemed to blame him all the same.

From the sound of her grunting and the weakness of her chopping, it was going to take her forever to get rid of the plant. As she chopped, Ruth's piercing grumbling was constant and agonising. Zelie longed for the relief that might come from blocking her ears but her fingers were too frozen even inside her pockets to expose them to the cold open air. The only thing that kept her there was the dwindling possibility that the beans were unharmed. Who knew how trampled down that earth would be now? And Ruth might very well be standing on the very spot she had dropped them, pressing them further into the cold dirt.

When Zelie thought she could take it no longer, Auntie Ruth let out a sudden great curse and, with a thump, threw down the axe. "A blister! You ungrateful stupid waste of metal and wood. I'll turn your handle into toothpicks and melt down your head for horseshoes. Silly sodding excuse for a…"

There was a squeak then a boom as the door slammed and the windowpanes rattled and the horrible voice of Auntie Ruth became a distant mumble.

Zelie shivered, crossed her arms across her chest and breathed out a misty sigh. Without knowing it, she had been holding her breath to stay quiet. A breeze blew away the frosty air but the cold seemed to have crept into the deepest part of her. The warmth of those beans would feel heavenly right now.

All was quiet now except for the slow drip of thawing ice falling from the huge leaves. She had to make a move now. She did not want to be in the garden after dark again. Auntie Ruth would be sufficiently distracted with her blister for a while and, though Sawyer might see her on his way to wherever the hog house might be, Zelie was unconcerned.

With a deep breath she began to climb. It was more difficult this time. Her shivering arms and frozen fingers made it almost impossible to maintain a firm grip on the slippery branches. Twice, she lost her footing and feared she might fall. But through sheer will, she held on and continued to climb.

When she reached the top of the fence, a quick

glance around the garden showed no threat so she allowed her hungry gaze to seek out the beans. The broom was still embedded halfway up the fence where Auntie Ruth had tried to spear her yesterday. The abandoned axe lay below it beside a series of shallow scars in the side of the plant's stem. Auntie Ruth had done very little damage with all that chopping. Zelie had thought she might see a hint of a blue glow or some other trace of the beans, but there was nothing. Even the gnomes had disappeared.

She perched on the top of the fence, scowling, breathing warmth into her hands and wishing she had brought a thicker sweater. But she was not ready to give up yet. She needed to take a closer look.

The leaf pile was flattened to the point she was certain it would not cushion another jump from the top of the fence. Rising up in front of her, the mysterious plant spiralled into the sky, waving side to side in the breeze, teasing her. Its deep green stems appeared glossy and smooth, like slippery plastic, pressing against one another to form a groove that coiled down into the earth in a way that suddenly gave Zelie an idea. Why not ride the spiral down to the ground?

With a smile, she crouched on top of the old fence. Its rickety frame creaked and swayed backwards uncooperatively. But before it could overcome her balance, she hopped onto the plant.

At first she perched motionless with her shoes wedged in the slippery groove between the stems. But it only took a small wriggle to set her hands and shoes sliding along and down its slick surface. As she eased into motion, a smile pricked at her mouth. Slowly, she rode the spiral, around and down, then a little faster. Around and down. She was buzzing inside.

The wind rose in her ears. Faster she spun and faster

until there was nothing she could do to slow down. The world was a grey and green blur. It felt like the time she was on the playground round-a-bout on her first day of school and a boisterous boy from year six had spun it so hard that she thought she was going to die. If not for a teacher who heard her screams and pulled the boy away, she might have been flung off into the climbing bars or against the wall.

But there was no one to save her today. Zelie grimaced as she fought to hold her body inwards. Her fingers and arms burned and quivered under the strain. Around, down, around, down, faster and faster and faster.

She gave a squeal as one foot, then the other lost hold and flicked outwards, pulling her fingers away from the slippery stem and sending her into a perilous tumble through the air. The world went silent except for her thumping heart. Then with a brutal jolt, she rebounded off the fence and then landed on her back with a force that emptied her lungs. She slid down the side of the leaf pile until her head pressed a dent into the soft ground.

Gasping for air, she cleared her face of leaves with one hand. Her other arm was useless. From elbow to hand, it was filled with a pain that ached, tickled and itched all at once. Rolling onto the good elbow, she breathed in straining, painful whoops. Stars danced in front of her eyes and her breakfast threatened to make a reappearance.

After a few seconds, she heaved a great lungful of air and fell into a coughing fit that lasted a full minute. At the end of it, she flopped on her back, eyes closed and chest rising and falling rapidly. How lucky she had been not to land flat on the ground or on that axe. It could have been much worse.

Her short moment of peace was interrupted by a twitch in her aching arm. Adrenaline, she hoped. But again it twitched and ached and a shaky sense of worry came over her. The plaster cast had only come off that arm two months ago. Beth would be distraught if Zelie had broken it again so soon. To her relief, the tingling feeling in her arm seemed to be subsiding.

The words 'funny bone' had just popped into her head when a violet blow sent the same arm off the leaf pile and onto the grass above her head. She shrieked and found herself standing upright in the clearing without realising how she got there. On instinct, she brushed off her arm, shoulder and back. A stray leaf tickled her neck and made her jump about to dislodge it. "Errghck!" she yelled.

"Heh heh, look at her dancing," chuckled a deep voice that sent Zelie wheeling around to the face the leaf pile.

"Not much of a singer though," said another voice.

"Is someone? —who said that?" Zelie said, stumbling a little. She felt lightheaded after standing up too quickly.

"It was Thurin," said a higher pitched voice. "But only because it was his turn to speak."

"And now it's time for Dresden to talk again!" boomed original speaker with such resonance that it made the leaves quiver.

"Too loud," hissed the first two voices—a warning which made Zelie suddenly aware that she was standing in the open garden and easily seen if Auntie Ruth happened to be looking through the window. She cast a fleeting glance at the house. It was silent but, just to be sure, she took a few precautionary steps towards the fence before returning her attention to the leaf pile and the puzzle of hidden voices.

Four small fingers of a white-gloved hand curled out through the leaves and pushed them aside like a panel window. A small terracotta man with a hole in its cheek and a faded red hat peeked out at her, an expression of concern printed onto his filth-smudged face. Zelie recognised him as the gnome that had fallen on its side by the fence last night. Zelie rubbed her eyes and blinked in astonishment as the gnome's eyes flicked heedfully around the garden. Seeming satisfied, the print on the gnomes face flickered into a smile and its gaze snapped up at Zelie so suddenly that she took a step backwards.

"Sorry I kicked your arm away so roughly," said the grimy gnome. He trudged out of the leaf pile and unstuck the leaves from his body as if to clean himself. But that only revealed yet more filth. Under the smeared dirt, his shirt, trousers and boots were painted in the same faded red as his hat.

"It's just that you were squashing us," said the higher pitched voice from inside the leaf pile.

"We would have called your name," said the deeper voice. "But we don't know it yet."

"Speaking of names," said the red gnome clearing his throat and holding out a dirt-smeared hand to shake. "I'm Thurin. And you are?"

# CHAPTER FIVE

## *Strange New Friends*

Zelie blinked at the red gnome who had just appeared from the leaf pile. "Your n-name is Thurin?" she stammered, in a state of shock.

As the terracotta man nodded, the edges of the hole in his cheek reflected the light. She could see right into his hollow body. Abandoned cobwebs laced with dust, jiggled with the movement of his head.

"And you are?" Thurin repeated.

Zelie's mouth moved wordlessly. She could not believe what she was seeing. And in that moment, for some reason, she could not speak her name. Instead, a series of vowels streamed out of her mouth with no meaning whatsoever.

The red gnome shook his head and muttered: "well, so much for manners." Then he cupped his grimy white glove to his mouth and spoke towards the leaf pile. "All clear you two. Come on out."

"Hello," said the high-pitched voice, as another gnome popped out of the pile sending a clump of leaves into Zelie's face. Zelie wiped them away with both hands. She was briefly aware that the arm she had hurt was obviously unimpaired. But her relief was fleeting as her brain devoted its energy to wrestling with the idea that gnomes could come to life and start speaking to people. This gnome was a girl who wore a small powdery green hat and matching frilly dress.

"Let's take a closer look," boomed the third voice,

before its owner burst into view. This gnome was plump and wore faded blue clothing and an expression of merry curiosity. He grabbed the green girl gnome's hand and led her out next to Thurin. "It's that girl from last night—the climber."

All the gnomes appeared to be in a very poor state. Their paint had become dull with age and their hats and noses were covered in cracks and chips, though none as fresh as Thurin's cheek. They looked ancient, but jostled for position with all the energy of children lining up for a turn on a slippery dip. The girl gnome twitched and bounced on her toes with excitement, waving hello with a flutter of her hand that gave the impression that her elbow was glued to her dress.

"It's so good to meet another girl. We're going to be such good friends. I'm Bre."

"Like the cheese," said the blue gnome, with a hearty chuckle that made his belly bounce.

"Except that it's short for Brienz," Thurin said sternly, giving the blue gnome a swift elbow in the ribs. "And *his* name is Dresden."

At the announcement of his name, the chubby gnome beamed under his blue hat with his hips set proudly forward so his belly poked right out like a pincushion.

"Doesn't talk much does she?" Dresden said behind his hand. But his voice was so loud and clear that he might have saved himself the trouble of trying to hide it.

And then a curious thing happened. The gnomes began a run of words in which they all took turns talking. But they swapped so quickly that there was never even time for a breath between sentences.

"Suppose it's good that she's quiet," started Thurin.

"Because if we were loud," continued Bre.

"Old Auntie Iceberg would come out," said

Dresden.

"And if she notices a big gnome like this in her garden."

"She'll smash her into tiny pieces."

"You're the biggest garden gnome we've *ever* seen."

"Me?" Zelie attempted to clarify. But the gnomes continued without stopping.

"You must be from the giant's garden."

"That's why you're so big. Well, big for a gnome, anyway."

"Everything would have to be huge up there."

"The mice must be the size of horses!"

"And the pigeons. Oh, think of the mess they must leave."

"Do you talk much with the giant?"

"What do you mean, *the giant*?" Zelie blurted, not understanding at all what they were talking about.

"He doesn't say much either, does he?"

All at once the gush of words stopped pouring from the gnomes and they were still as stone. The only movement from them was the slow widening of their eyes.

"Quick. Hide," they said in unison.

"What?" said Zelie.

"Can't you hear? Sawyer's coming." The gnomes began to run on their tiny legs back to the leaf pile.

With a few quick strides, Zelie overtook them and crouched behind the pile. Something small and shining on the ground caught her eye. She had already picked it up and put it in her pocket before she realised it was not the magic bean she was hoping for.

Sawyer appeared through a doorway. Bent in self-pity, he hugged a small pillow and a blanket and scuffed his boots all the way to a distant shed which Zelie guessed was the hog house.

"Um, gnomes," said Zelie, remembering the reason she had returned to the garden. "Thank you for the, um, greeting," she began, trying not to sound uncomfortable addressing a trio of garden gnomes.

"You're welcome," they said in concert, shuffling and elbowing each other to be seen.

"I saw that you were all here last night."

"Yes, we saw you too," the gnomes replied together.

"Well, did you happen to see the magic beans I dropped?"

The gnomes exchanged knowing glances.

"So you *have* seen them?" Zelie said, clapping her hands.

"Oh yes, we saw the beans," nodded the blue gnome.

"OK, good. Um, it's Dresden isn't it?" Zelie said.

The blue gnome nodded.

"Do you think you could tell me where they are?"

The gnomes drew a simultaneous breath and then started speaking at such a rate, and swapping with such frequency, that Zelie felt lightheaded trying to keep up. It was like watching a movie on double the normal playing speed. But from somewhere inside the babble, Zelie learned two of the beans had landed on the ground and the other fell through the hole in Thurin's cheek.

"I guess Auntie Ruth didn't stomp those two beans hard enough into the ground," Bre said.

"In fact, she must have buried them to just the right depth," Dresden continued.

"It was only a minute after Ruth went inside that we saw the two little green heads of the beanstalk poke out of the ground," Thurin said.

"Beanstalk?" Zelie said.

"Yes," Bre said, pointing at the coiled plant. "As you

can see, it wasn't a sprout for long."

"A beanstalk?" Zelie repeated, following Bre's finger.

"*Beanstalks* really—there's two of them wound together as if they had been spun on a potters wheel."

"And they're noisier than you might think."

"But the old girl didn't hear anything."

"Or see anything."

"She must have been angrier than usual."

"Which is very lucky because if she had seen that big hole in Thurin's cheek, he would be a pile of pebbles by now."

"Indeed," Thurin said, gruffly, pointing at the hole in his face. "There was no need for this. I mean, jumping onto leaf piles. Disgraceful behaviour."

"I didn't mean to," Zelie said, raising a hand in apology. Thurin recoiled with a snort.

"Oh, don't pay any attention to old grumble bum," said Bre. "The magic bean would have bounced right off him if it weren't for that hole. Then we might have had a beanstalk made of three stems. And none of us would be talking right now."

"And I wouldn't be able to do this." Dresden gave his middle a sharp prod, which sent a rubbery belly blob revolving around and around his body. "Ho, ho! Look at it go!" he chuckled, moving his hips in a hula hoop fashion.

Zelie scratched her head. "Wait. There are two beanstalks. From two beans right? But you said the third one dropped inside the hole in Thurin's cheek. So… do you think I could have it back?" Zelie asked, hopefully.

"Nope," huffed Thurin.

"Why not?"

"It's gone," said Bre.

"Gone? Where?" Zelie said anxiously.

"The magic got absorbed."

"By me."

"Then me."

"And then me," Dresden said, still hula hooping his belly around and around. "That's how I got this groove on, baby."

"Alright, enough with the blubber dance," said Thurin.

Though it was an amusing sight, Zelie barely smiled. She felt the urge to curl up on the ground. The beans were gone. She would never feel their warmth and see their patterns again. She would never know the possibilities they held or the wonders they might reveal. She let her eyes drift off into the darkening distance. Night was falling again. The world felt like it was closing in around her, squeezing out all hope.

She was barely aware that the gnomes, oblivious to her pain, had launched into another cooperative story, this one describing their first sensations after the magic took effect.

"I was tingly and warm all over," Thurin was saying.

"But he had never walked before."

"So he stumbled-"

"All over the place-"

"Like a baby giraffe-"

"A dizzy one-"

"With only three legs."

"And when Thurin tripped over-"

"He bumped into Bre-"

"Who fell on Dresden."

"That bean had too much magic for any of us to hold."

"It kept on spilling over."

"I nudged an earthworm with my toe earlier."

"You should have seen that little guy burrow."

"It rained dirt for about a minute," finished Dresden.

All three gnomes laughed.

Suddenly, they fell silent. It was jarring. The gnomes seemed to have spoken almost continuously since Zelie had met them. So when they stopped, it was as if she had suddenly gone deaf. All three gnomes were staring —not straight at her, but at her hair—and each wore a very different expression. Dresden appeared to be stifling a laugh. Thurin's face held a look of dread. And Bre was squeaking and hopping from foot to foot, hands clasped tightly as if her excitement were trapped inside them and would escape if she let go.

"What is it? What are you looking at?"

"Look at it glow," the gnomes all said together.

Zelie thought perhaps they meant 'look at it go' and began feeling around on her head, trying to find what the fuss was all about. To her bemusement, a faint tinkling sound rang out each time she touched at the top of her head, triggering diverse reactions from the gnomes. Reaching for one of her straggly plaits, Zelie found instead what felt like a heavy silken scarf. On instinct, she gave it a sharp tug only to find it was firmly attached to her scalp, the force of the pull doing nothing but to bend her head to one side. It was not a strip of heavy silk. It was her hair. But how could it be?

In a blink, she had its silky strands drawn over her shoulder to see with her own eyes. It was at least triple its normal length and as soft as velvet. But while that was a surprise enough—considering she had never given it the care and attention needed for such a result —its softness and length was not her greatest concern. After all, hair could be soft and silky with the right treatment. But what hair could not possibly do under any circumstance was to emit light. But somehow that was exactly what hers was doing. Glimmering waves the colour of candlelight were travelling up and down each strand.

"What is this?" she muttered, as much to herself than anyone else, as she stared into its hypnotic glow. It was Bre who offered an answer.

"It's delightful. Wonderful. Oh I wish mine were just like it."

"Ah, yes, it's lovely and very, er—melodic," said Thurin awkwardly. "But it does make you stand out quite a bit. And if you have been listening to anything we have said, you will understand that things that attract attention don't last very long around here."

"Well, it doesn't have an off switch," snapped Zelie. "Just let me think for a moment?" It was all coming together. The beans. The flashes. The basin of water. It was magic. Just as the gnomes had harnessed the swirling mystical power of the bean she had dropped in the garden, her hair had received some sort of enchantment from the bean that dissolved in the basin. Glowing hair was hardly something she might have wished for. But, until the magic wore off, she would not need to carry a flashlight. At least that was something.

"Thurin's right," said Dresden. "You might like to think somewhere else. If Auntie Ruth comes out, she won't hesitate to put your lights out, permanently."

"Alright. Alright. Big scary Auntie Ruth. I get it. I was just trying to understand this and maybe enjoy it for a couple of seconds. It's not every day you find out that you have magic in your hair."

As Zelie flicked her hair over her shoulders, she felt a tickle in her scalp as if a bird was nibbling it. Her hands went automatically to her head to shoo it away, but instead of feathers and a beak, her hands found a newly weaved braid that extended to two neat plaits.

"Now that's more like it," Zelie said with a smile. "Bye bye hairbrushes and bobby pins."

Bre's eyes were so wide, Zelie was sure her eyeballs were going to roll out and go bouncing across the ground in different directions. But the other gnomes did not share the same excitement. Instead, they exchanged furrowed expressions and shuffled their feet.

As if to ease their worry, an earthy melody bloomed out of nowhere and rose into the night air. It was the sweetest and most moving tune Zelie had ever heard.

"What's that music? Oh, it's so beautiful. Where is it coming from?" Zelie murmured, glancing around the dark garden in slow wonder. The melody was filled with such aching longing, like the voices of two souls who longed to be one.

"Oh it's just the beanstalks," Thurin said, gesturing at the spiralling plant. "Weren't you just leaving?"

"Oh, just the beanstalks. Of course, it's so ordinary." Zelie did not mean to be snarky but something about his casual dismissal annoyed her. She could see by the glow of her hair that what he said was true enough. As the two stems coiled ever tighter and taller, they thrummed a slow dreamy duet. Waving gently, the leaves seemed to bid her a slow farewell before fading out of sight into the shadow of night above.

Like fingernails on a chalkboard, Auntie Ruth's voice cut through the tranquility.

"Who's got music on? Turn it off. This isn't a disco."

Zelie's stomach did a cartwheel. Her anxious gaze fell on the axe. Auntie Ruth had tried to spear Zelie with a broom handle last night. Would she be so quick to take up the axe if she found Zelie in her garden for the second night in a row?

The latch and bolt clanked behind the kitchen door as Ruth fumbled to open it. Zelie picked up the axe and hid it behind the beanstalk. But there was no way to hide while her hair was shining an orange halo on the fence.

"Sawyer, you pile of vomit. You've bungled up this latch."

"Oh my gosh, what do I do? She's going see me," Zelie whispered, grimacing. "And what if she sees you with your cheek like that, Thurin?"

"Don't worry about us. We'll find a place to hide. You'd better hurry back to the giant's garden," Thurin whispered, gesturing for her to climb the beanstalk. "Stay down here and she'll stomp you to powder."

Zelie frowned and shook her head. Thurin still thought her to be a gnome. Why? And what was all that talk about a giant and his garden? Zelie would have loved to ask all those questions and more, but there was no time.

She clambered up the twisted fence towards safety. The plant hummed her a sonorous departing tune. The shuffle of wet leaves indicated the gnomes were back inside the leaf pile. Ruth was still battling with the latch as Zelie hopped over the top of the fence and stood on one of the gnarled protrusions on the other side for one final word. "Good bye," she called.

"Wait," said Bre as three leafy patches moved aside like tiny windows revealing the gnomes' concerned faces gazing up at Zelie. "We never got your name."

The angry voice muffled louder from inside and the clunk and clank of the lock and latch became more urgent.

"It's Zelie. And, by the way, I'm not a gnome."

"Then you must be a small human," boomed Dresden. His words reverberated around the garden and Zelie heard a clink as one of the other gnomes clapped a hand over Dresden's mouth.

Just then the door of the house burst open and Zelie let go of the fence.

"What is that racket?" rattled the voice.

Zelie whistled through the air. She landed and rolled smoothly onto her feet and in the same motion, began running away down the alley. For the second time this week, she escaped into the night. Only this time the alley was bathed in the warm glow of her magic hair. Her heavy plaits bounced from side to side tinkling and the rusty voice faded into the darkening alley behind her.

Lying in bed, Zelie inspected the glinting object she had picked up at the base of the fence and determined that it was the missing piece of Thurin's cheek. Ever since the gnomes suggested that Ruth would crush Thurin to pebbles if she saw the hole in his cheek, she had felt a queasy feeling in her stomach. With Dresden's megaphone voice, she thought there was a good chance she would find them tomorrow. But if Zelie could fix Thurin's cheek with some glue before she noticed, Thurin might be spared. "That settles it," she said to herself. "I'll go back first thing in the morning." Perhaps Thurin would finally forgive her if she did a good enough job.

Zelie reached over to switch off her lamp but it was already off.

# CHAPTER SIX

## *Curious Jack*

Zelie was not the type of person who liked lazy mornings in bed. She liked to get up and start her day early. So when she awoke at noon with something very important to do, she was doubly frustrated.

"It's so late," she kept muttering, as she wrestled herself into mismatched clothes. "Why is it so late?"

Last night, the glow of her hair was as bright as a hundred candles. Her fascination with it soon gave way to frustration when she realised there was no way to turn it off. With her eyes closed everything looked bright red. That would have been enough to keep her awake all on its own. But it got worse. Every time she shifted her head, even an inch, her hair chimed like a harp. By the time she got up to find a thick scarf to warp around her head and found a position where she could hold deathly still, her mind would not be silenced. Instead, it juggled the untold mysteries of magic and waltzed with the memory of the beanstalks' sweet tune. When sleep finally took hold, it locked her tightly inside a dark and dreamless carriage from which she did not escape until midday.

It was a Saturday, which explained why Beth thought it was OK to leave her sleeping. But fixing the hole in Thurin's cheek seemed more important than school. It felt like saving a life. She could not afford to waste time.

"Come on. Come on," she urged as she filled her

backpack. She would never forgive herself if Auntie Ruth smashed Thurin into little pieces just because of her clumsiness and, now, laziness.

Despite their ceaseless chatter, Zelie could not help liking the gnomes. So much so, that she was going to break one of her firm rules. Zelie cleaned for nobody. But there was something about those gnomes that made her want to keep them safe. And that meant making sure that Auntie Ruth had no reason to do them any harm. From the look of the rest of the garden, it was only a matter of time before Ruth decided the gnomes were too dirty or damaged to remain. And so today, Zelie would make a necessary exception.

Still muttering, she ran out to her father's old workshop to collect glue, rags and other supplies.

*

At first the heavy drawer of the old filing cabinet inched open, squealing as it awoke from years of hibernation. Then it held firm in an obstinate grin. Zelie could see the glue and some of the paints inside, but the gap was too small to fit her hand. And no matter how much Zelie pulled, kicked, yanked and yelled, the gap refused to widen. In Zelie's tired state, frustration took an easy hold. A cramp in her hand was enough to bring her efforts to a screaming halt. She plopped down next to the cabinet, sending up a cloud of fine dust.

After the inevitable coughing fit, she rested her back against the cabinet and allowed herself to marinate in her own misery. She had not realised that her eyelids were closed until a whistled tune roused her.

It was a familiar melody and a particularly welcome one today. Jack: if he could not open the drawer then nobody could. But Zelie would have to make it quick. Once Jack got talking, he had a way of getting secrets out of Zelie. Normally, this would cause only mild frustration but the events of the last few days were not for sharing. And if there was one thing that could send Jack into a longwinded rant, it was news of children using magic.

It was not the lecture she feared: the Mayor-this and the Authorities-that. Jack talked—to everyone—all the time. He could not help it. Even if his heart was in the right place. Even if he tried to protect Zelie from getting into trouble, he would end up saying something to the wrong person.

Just then, a shadow moved past the window and in that moment of darkness, Zelie's hair gave out a brief tinkle and a pulse of orange light. Her stomach lurched.

"Is that you Squirrel?" Jack said, peeking through the glass.

Zelie felt the goosebumps rise up on her arms as she wrestled the hood of her jacket into place over her incandescent hair.

"What's that you're hiding?"

Zelie drew in a sharp breath. "Umm… it's…"

Jack might be able to get away with growing a magic pumpkin. But for some reason, children were dealt with particularly harshly when it came to illegal use of magic. Even a charmed rhinestone, as simple as it was, cost that boy a year in prison and turned him into a mumbling mess. What sort of treatment would glowing hair receive? Government scientists would be very interested. An image of a dissected frog floating in a jar flashed through Zelie's mind.

Jack moved away from the window. The light that flowed in and extinguished the glow of her hair was little comfort as his footsteps circled around the outside of the shed towards the door. Heat rose to Zelie's cheeks. If only she knew a spell to make herself disappear. Searching her thoughts for some sort of excuse, she found no ideas, only more terrifying images. This time, her own head, shaved bald and marked with purple lines and crosses as she lay still on an operating table. Then, in her mind, she was climbing out a window and running through tangled thickets, scared, cold, and alone.

Jack appeared in the doorway, a look of concern on his face. "So, Lass. What's the story?"

"Nothing," insisted Zelie, still stretching her hood down to her eyebrows. Her insides seemed to have engaged in an all-in brawl.

"Squirrel. I know you better than that. Come on. Spill the beans."

Beans? Did he already know? "I don't want to talk about it. OK? Just leave me alone. OK?"

"Whoah. Turn down the flames, Squirrel. I'm charcoal. And don't scowl at me. If the wind changes you will be stuck like that—Silent treatment eh? Fine then, I'll do the talking. Look, I understand. A girl's gotta have her secrets. Twelve years old and all that-"

"Thank you."

"But, that don't mean it's safe to go messing about with magic," lectured Jack.

"I know. Everybody knows. But why?"

"Because it's unreliable and illegal."

"But you use it."

"For special reasons and in controlled conditions."

"Like growing giant pumpkins in your front garden?" Zelie said, widening her eyes.

"Well not exactly. You know it could have been worse. You should have seen—" he started and then laughed. "There I go again. Me and my mouth! Forgive me Squirrel, but we can't talk about this. In fact, we shouldn't even talk about *not* talking about it."

Zelie shook her head.

"It's for your own good, Lass. The laws are there for a reason and the authorities don't go easy on kids. You don't need that kind of strife."

Zelie sighed in resignation. But Jack seemed to be waiting for some sort of assurance. It was exasperating.

"OK. I understand," she said, folding her arms.

"You'll have to do better than that, Squirrel."

"I'll be careful."

"Careful eh? Well that might have to do for today," Jack said and straightened. "It might surprise you to hear that I didn't come round to chat. According to your Mum, your garden has more slugs than salad. I'm here to put this green thumb of mine to work. "

"Before you go," said Zelie, remembering the drawer. "I could do with some help too."

Jack's gaze dropped to the palm of Zelie's hand where she was absently massaging a freshly formed blister. "Aye aye. So what's your pickle?"

"I need to get this open," Zelie said, rapping her knuckles on the outside of the cabinet. "Do you think you could give it a try?"

"I've got just the thing for that," he said rolling up his sleeves. "Spriggins' all-purpose elbow grease—extra strength."

Zelie stood back as Jack took hold of the drawer and pulled. It did not budge. He tugged harder and harder, until eventually he had both feet on the cabinet and was heaving with all his might and weight. Suddenly, his fingers slipped sending him flying across the workshop into a pile of wooden planks, which fell into a heap on top of him.

"Oh my gosh. Are you alright?" Zelie asked, rushing over to him.

"It's nothing," Jack coughed. The wood clattered to the floor as he stood and straightened his jacket. "This is a pickle indeed," he said.

"Well, thanks for trying Jack," said Zelie as she dusted off his shoulders.

"Oh, I'm not done, Squirrel. You know I can't turn my back on a lady in need. After all, there's few men-"

"-as gallant as Mr Jack Spriggins," said Zelie, finishing Jack's sentence with a roll of her eyes. It was one of his more common claims.

"Truer words've never been spoken," Jack said with a bow.

Zelie smiled. "So how's the view from your high horse?"

Jack looked at Zelie with an expression of proud shock. "Using me own sayings against me? Well I never. It's like being smacked with me own spade." He pointed a finger skyward and said: "and speaking of long-handled tools, I'd better consult me crowbar about this little dilemma. I'll go get it right now." In a few long strides he left through the doorway. "Be back in two shakes of a lamb's tail," he called over his shoulder. "Maybe three."

Jack was not known for finishing jobs quickly. The fact that he had dismissed whatever gardening work he was supposed to be doing was a sign that today he was particularly susceptible to distraction. 'Two shakes' could take hours; days even. Hopefully Thurin had the sense to stay out of Auntie Ruth's sight. But if not, that hole would be easy to spot. There was no time for waiting.

"Isn't there a quicker way?" Zelie cried after Jack and immediately regretted it because her hair seemed to answer her by giving off a chime.

Jack spun around and shot her a curious glance. Then he ambled back to the doorway, hands in pockets and a sparkle in his eye. "A quicker way? Like what?"

"I don't know," she said nervously, willing her hair to stay quiet.

Jack wore a curious look. "Well, now I think about it, we could fashion a lever from a few of those wooden planks and some glue or—that'll do, there's some nails over on that bench. You know where I can get my hands on a hammer?"

"No. And I don't have time to *fashion a lever*, Jack. I can't wait. I just want the drawer open."

A quiver shot through Zelie's scalp. The hood of her jacket fell down against her back and an orange glow eased onto Jack's gaping face. Glimmering wisps appeared into view from behind her, waving in the air, as if flowing in some mysterious current. By the time she realised it was her own hair, it had weaved itself into several thick cords above her head which wafted towards the cabinet and coiled around the drawer handle like octopus's tentacles. Then, slowly, and with a chilling squeak, the drawer slid open. The tentacles unravelled from the handle, retraced their wavy journey back over Zelie's head and collapsed gently against her back. Finally, with a twitch, the glow was gone.

"Well, colour me pink, Squirrel." Jack gave a whistle of admiration and then he snapped out of his boyish trance and checked his watch. "For fifteen minutes you listened to me prattle on about not using magic. And that whole time you had that heavy-duty hair-do under your hood?"

"Yes," Zelie said, with a guilty smirk. "It wasn't planned, Jack. It was sort of an accident," Zelie said, pulling up the hood of her jacket.

Jack shook his head, gave a grimace and turned one shoulder towards the door. She had seen that look before.

"Please don't tell my mother."

"Alright I won't."

"Or anyone else. Please Jack. Just this once. Let it be our secret."

Jack chewed his bottom lip and studied Zelie as she took off her backpack and unzipped it to put the drawer's contents inside.

"Please?" Zelie begged.

"Alright Lass, I'll try to keep me trap shut, so long as you keep your wits about you." He tapped a finger on his temple.

"I will," Zelie promised, as she gathered up paints and brushes from inside the drawer and piled them into her bag.

"Keep that shiny noggin hidden and don't forget, you promised me that you would be careful," Jack said as she kissed him on the cheek and rushed out the door.

"I'll be fine."

"Keep the sun in your heart, Squirrel," Jack said grimly, but she was already gone.

# CHAPTER SEVEN

## *Zelie meets Sawyer*

In Zelie's backpack, the bottle of detergent gurgled and the paints and brushes rattled against her lunchbox as she climbed the twisted fence again. She knew the climb well now and her hands and feet found their way easily.

A confusing mixture of excitement and fear swirled inside her. What was this strange magic inside her hair? The bells, the glow, the extraordinary strength? It opened a drawer that Jack could not even budge. As twice winner of the Annual Emerson Boulder Throwing Competition, he was probably the strongest man on the island. For a moment, she wondered how well her hair might toss a boulder. It seemed to have a mind of its own at times. It lit up whenever it got dark and sounded like a miniature wind chime whenever it moved. Not to mention the fact that it performed feats of strength at the mere mention of an obstacle. Jack said something about magic being dangerous and unreliable. Unpredictable might be a better word. But what else did he know about magic that caused him to grow a freak pumpkin one day and to worry about magic hair on another? Jack's voice rang out in her head: 'keep your wits about you'. It was his way of reminding her not to get caught up in daydreams like this one.

She reached the top of the fence, this time having resolved to be sensible and climb down the beanstalk instead of spinning down its slippery coils. But she had

53

been so preoccupied with her thoughts about Jack and her glowing hair, she had not noticed what, again, should have been plainly obvious. The tall, thin, bendy plant she had seen yesterday was gone. In its place was a mighty pillar of timber at least twenty times its previous girth. A thick winding column of rough oak-like wood stood before her. The two trunks were wound together so tightly that the spiral she had ridden yesterday was almost indiscernible and each of the tree's leaves were now big enough to cover a large car. For some reason, she found the presence of this new mystery most frustrating.

"What is it with this weird garden?" she yelled at the column of wood.

From behind the wooden trunk, a boy's voice caught her by surprise. "Ah! Who's there? What do you want?"

Glancing down at the base of the mighty tree, she noticed the red gnome and the blue gnome, Thurin and Dresden, looking up at her. They were hiding from view. Thurin was mouthing words that Zelie could not read. She squinted to decipher his lips. "It's Sawyer... *Sawyer*," he seemed to be repeating, silently, as he pointed in the direction of the boy's voice.

So what? thought Zelie. She was not worried about Sawyer. "What about Auntie Ruth?" she whispered.

The gnomes exchanged glances. Dresden cupped a hand to his ear and shook his head.

Zelie crossed her arms across her chest and shivered, as if she were freezing.

Dresden opened his mouth and tapped his finger, knowingly, on the side of his head. "Gone out," said his lips.

"Well, that's a relief," Zelie exclaimed, audibly.

"Eep!" shrieked Sawyer. "Stop whoever you are. I

have a weapon. Don't come in here."

Zelie stepped sideways along the top of the fence to see. The boy was standing in the open, gripping something with both hands and pointing it defensively at various parts of the garden as if he expected an ambush but was unsure from which direction it would be coming.

Now that Zelie had an audience, climbing down the beanstalk seemed too dull. For some reason, she felt obliged to arrive in a more spectacular fashion. Her chest fluttered with excitement as an idea came to her. She grabbed one of the huge leaves that were lolling side to side above her head. It felt like soft thin leather between her fingers. Taking a small blade from her pocket, she sawed at the stem and pulled the leaf free. Then, grabbing each side of the leaf, she launched herself off the top of the fence.

She let out a shriek as the leaf ballooned above her like a parasail. Along the side wall of the house and past the wooden kitchen door she floated, circling around Sawyer and landing between him and the house wearing a huge smile.

A faint whimper leaked from between Sawyer's trembling lips. He was about Zelie's height and looked stocky and strong, despite his hunched posture. He wore baggy trousers, the knees heavy with mud, over an old pair of shoes with a hole in one of the toes. His faded blue jacket was caked with dark mud on one side as if he had been recently lying in muck. And inside the open zip, he wore a white shirt with a hole burned black in the middle. Sooty lines streaked outwards from the hole, up his neck and cheeks. Auntie Ruth had made good on her punishment, although whatever she had done to burn a hole in his shirt seemed particularly cruel. Clasped tightly in his sooty hands Sawyer held some sort of small brush with blue bristles.

"What are you doing in here?" he said, urgently, his green eyes aquiver under a heavy mop of brown hair.

"You mean, apart from performing that magnificent entrance?" Zelie said, feeling as if she should have received some sort of applause. "You're Sawyer aren't you?"

Sawyer gasped. "How do you know my—" His voice trailed off with a squeak and his face contorted in a way that gave Zelie the impression that he might cry. He straightened and held the brush up towards her with both hands. "No one is allowed inside the garden," he said, with unconvincing authority.

"Well, it's lucky I'm not no one. I'm Zelie. Pleased to—urgckh!" She had extended her hand to greet Sawyer but withdrew it quickly when the stench of burned flesh mixed with pig's muck reached her nostrils. "Maybe we'll shake hands later," Zelie said, pinching her nose closed.

"Later? No. You've got to leave. No one can be in here."

"Whatever," Zelie said rudely as she scanned the garden for the gnomes.

"I said, *go away*," Sawyer yelled with a weak two-handed jab of the brush. "Right now, or—or I'll have to use this."

"OK, calm down and put your toothbrush away. All I want to do is-"

"It will hurt, you know," Sawyer said, as he twisted the brush in the air. "It's magic," he whispered, as if it was a secret.

"Look, the only thing you're scaring is the plaque on my teeth."

"It's not a toothbrush. It can do terrible things. If you don't leave, I'll show you," Sawyer threatened, his voice wavering. Zelie suspected that Sawyer might be a little dim. But she resented being told off by someone her own age. She had had enough telling off from adults.

"Go on then, I want to see it."

To Zelie's astonishment, a tendril of her hair lashed out, coiled around the handle and snatched it from Sawyer's grip before he had a chance to react. After it had dropped the brush in her waiting hands, the tendril of hair went limp, swaying at knee-length. Sawyer opened and closed his mouth at his empty hands and then gave Zelie a look of astonished horror.

Zelie twirled the loose lock of hair around her finger, as if she had planned the whole thing, and flicked it over her back where it was ensnared and wound into some neat pattern with the rest of her hair.

Sawyer gasped. "Are you a witch?" he said in a fearful whisper.

"A witch? I think you've been reading too many fairy tales. What is this thing?"

Examining the brush, she noticed that what she had taken for bristles were more like translucent crystals poking from a long and tapered handle of dark grey metal. It was much heavier than she expected and, as dirty as it was, it shimmered in a way Zelie had never seen. Sawyer ducked and danced to avoid the bristled end as she examined it. She might have been waving around a gun the way he was carrying on.

"Hold still Sawyer, while I make your breath minty fresh," she said, hoping that a bit of humour might break the great wall of ice that seemed to have formed between them. But instead of laughing, Sawyer fell to his knees.

"Please don't hurt me. Oh p- please," he stammered with dribble bridging across his quivering lips.

"Oh jeez. I was just playing. Here, have it back. I

don't really want it. Just don't jab it at me like that. It's weird."

Sawyer got to his feet and approached gingerly, accepted the brush and took a step away. "So you're not a witch?"

"Of course not."

Sawyer flashed a worried glance at the top of her head. "How did you do that with your hair then? Is it magic?"

Zelie shrugged. "I suppose so. But it's not going to hurt you."

"That's just what a witch would say."

Zelie sighed. "Don't you have pigs to clean?"

Sawyer's forehead crinkled and he let out a strange bark like a sick dog. "You can read my mind. Oh no. Please no."

"No don't get on your knees again. I can't read your mind, Sawyer. Look, truthfully, I was hiding here in the garden last night. I heard you and your Auntie talking. That's how I knew about the pigs. Get up. Come on— That's it." She sighed while he rose from the ground, wiping the tears from his cheeks with a hasty hand, as if she might not notice. "Hey, I have an idea. Let's forget everything that just happened and act like we are meeting for the first time. Hi Sawyer. My name is Zelie. I'm not a witch. I just have some sort of magic in my hair. I can't hear what you're thinking or turn you into a toad or whatever. I knocked over one of the gnomes and I'm really sorry. I just wanted to come and fix him up." She decided not to say anything more about the gnomes and their new abilities for fear of spooking him further. This was even more delicate than talking to her mother.

Sawyer stared for a moment and then cleared his throat. "I'm Sawyer—and—and this is my house. We'll, my Auntie's, but I live here too—Sorry. I'm not used to meeting intruders."

"Intruders?"

"I- I mean visitors. Did you say you were here last night?"

"Yes," Zelie replied.

"You didn't see a paper bag out here somewhere did you?"

"No," Zelie lied.

"Oh," Sawyer muttered to himself. He sighed and stole a fleeting glance at the trunk of the beanstalk. "I guess they really are gone," he said to Zelie. Then after a thoughtful pause he said: "I'd better get to my chores then." He began to trudge towards the hog house, then hesitated and turned. "Um, Auntie will only be out for an hour or so. If you're still here when she gets back, please don't let her see you. She'll probably want to roast you in the oven."

"What? You mean she really eats people?" exclaimed Zelie.

"Or squashes them. At least that's what she says. We don't get many intruders—visitors, I mean," Sawyer said, as if the word 'intruders' was the most offensive thing he had said. "I gotta go do some cleaning now. You know—like you said." And with that half explanation Sawyer turned and moped away.

Zelie was still wrinkling her nose at the idea of roasting a person for dinner as Sawyer disappeared behind the stables.

"Is he gone?" came a little voice from the leaf pile.

"Gnomes," she exclaimed, rushing to the other side of the beanstalk. "Come with me. I have a surprise." She opened her bag. The trio of gnomes drifted out of the leaf pile towards her. "It's time you had a clean," she said, pulling a long cobweb from the hole in Thurin's cheek.

"You're very brave," Bre said.

"Oh, I'm not afraid of spiders," Zelie replied as she ran a foaming sponge over Thurin, wiping away years of grime.

"No, not because of that. Didn't that wand frighten you at all?" thundered Dresden. Zelie was pleased that Ruth was not home. Otherwise, she would certainly have heard Dresden's booming voice. Roast Zelie for dinner, she thought and shuddered.

"Did you say *wand*?"

"She doesn't know what it is?" tutted Thurin, lifting his arm for Zelie to clean under it.

"Know what *what* is?"

"How old would you be? Fifty?" Bre asked innocently.

"I'm twelve and a half!"

"Oh, so young," trumpeted Dresden. "No wonder you don't know anything."

Zelie poked the sponge at Dresden, leaving a ball of foam on his face. "I know things."

"But not about wands," Thurin said. "Have you heard of a unicorn?"

"A unicorn? Yes. It's a mythical horse with a horn on its nose," said Zelie, feeling as if she had passed some strange test of knowledge.

"They're not mythical or horses," said Bre. "Though they do share a likeness. Especially after losing their horns."

"Alright. So, apparently, I don't know about unicorns, OK? And I don't know about wands that look like toothbrushes, held by strange boys with nasty Aunties," Zelie said, rudely. There was an uncomfortable pause as all three gnomes placed their hands on their hips. "OK. OK. So unicorns look like horses. What's this got to do with Sawyer's toothbrush?"

The gnomes took this as encouragement for another run of words. They explained, in a very roundabout way, that every so often, a unicorn sheds its horn in the same way a human loses baby teeth. Most horns are flushed away by the fastest flowing rivers and end up in the deepest of oceans. So it is extremely rare to find one. But occasionally, one is churned up from the ocean depths and finds its way into the nets of a fishing trawler. And if such a horn sees the light of a full moon, it becomes a wand. And each full moon after that, the wand will sprout a single blue shard. Each shard allows one wish or spell.

Zelie laughed. "A full moon? What's that? Never mind. Hold still Thurin," she said as she glued his cheek back on with a rough prod. Next Zelie used a paintbrush and stroked bright lines of green paint onto Bre's faded hat.

"Ooohh," cooed the other two gnomes, watching the rich colour replace the hazy green beneath. Bre smiled proudly and performed a slow turn.

"OK. So, Sawyer has a wand, not a toothbrush," Zelie said, trying to get the gnomes back on track. "But why should that frighten anyone?"

"The wand only works for selfless spells," Dresden explained.

"Which means you can't just wish for something *you* want," continued Thurin.

"It has to be a spell that helps someone else."

"But if you *try* a selfish spell, like Sawyer, the wand shoots out a bolt of lightning."

"Lightning? Like real lightning, as in a storm?" Zelie said incredulously.

The gnomes nodded. "From both ends. Like this."

Thurin held up an imaginary wand at Dresden. Both

gnomes shook their bodies as if electricity was running through each of them.

"Sawyer doesn't know so he keeps making wishes for himself."

"You don't want to be around when he does it."

"You might get struck by the lightning from the other end."

Zelie remembered the soot on Sawyer's sweater, hands and neck. "Is that why he looks like he's been cuddling a burning log?" She was painting Bre's hair as a bout of laughter shook the little gnome, dislodging a blond-coloured blob from the paintbrush. It landed on Bre's shoulder. Bre watched sorrowfully as the blob of paint made a wavy yellow track down her green dress and onto her shoe.

"Oops," said Zelie. "Sorry, I'm not much of a painter."

The next moment, a blinding white flash lit up the entire garden. Whipping around, Zelie caught sight of a mighty vein of lightning shooting diagonally into the sky. Boom went the thunder followed by Sawyer's distant shriek. The windows and doors on the house rattled and a black cloud of smoke rose up into the air behind the stables.

"He's done it again," Bre said. Then she laughed. "Oh gosh, look at Thurin."

In Zelie's shock, she had squeezed the tube she was holding, sending a streak of blond coloured paint at Thurin. A horizontal yellow stripe now ran across his eyes like a domino mask. Thurin blinked through the paint.

"He's like a yellow Zorro," chuckled Dresden.

Thurin's eyes widened beneath his freshly painted mask and he pointed over Zelie's shoulder. "Look out. Burning boy coming in hot," he said.

Sawyer was running across from the pig shed, leaving a trail of smoke behind him. The centre of his sweater was now a burned hole with glowing edges, like the end of a candlewick just after it is blown out. His face was completely black and his sooty hair spiked up in the air. Still holding the wand, he ran to the water tap on the wall and splashed his chest over and over until his clothes stopped fizzing.

"What happened to you?" called Zelie.

Sawyer trudged over shaking his head. He was clutching his chest through the hole in his clothes. His eyes were bright against the black of his sooty face. In a temper, he threw down the wand. It embedded—handle-first—into the damp ground.

"That thing is totally useless."

"Looks like it could come in handy if you run out of matches," laughed Zelie, expecting the gnomes to join in. But they were silent. They seemed to have frozen into their original poses.

"It must be broken," complained Sawyer. "I didn't ask for lightning. I asked for the pigs to be clean."

"I don't think you're using it properly," Zelie said, as she pulled the wand from the ground with a slurp.

Sawyer yelped, leapt over the gnomes and trotted behind the beanstalk. "Don't play with it. You don't even know what it is," he said from behind the beanstalk.

"I bet I can get it working."

Sawyer poked his head out from behind the tree. "Put it down. It's not something you can fix. You're gonna get hurt."

"Clean!" Zelie shouted, pointing the wand at Sawyer's protruding head. The wand gave a sharp sniff, then a burst of stars exploded from the end. They curled around Sawyer like a net, pulling him from his hiding place and holding him in the air above the gnomes. Zelie giggled as Sawyer tried, in vain, to swim back to the beanstalk. She made a slow circle with the end of the wand and Sawyer turned head over heels inside the cloud. As he spun, soot and dust spilled off him and onto the gnomes below him. She waved the wand in another, faster circle. Sawyer whinnied as he turned another somersault and then another and another until the gnomes were half buried in a mound of grey-black dust.

Zelie let the wand drop to her side. The star cloud disappeared and Sawyer plopped down on the ground in front of the gnomes, skin shining, teeth gleaming, hair fluffy and his clothes spotless. Even the edge of the burned hole in his t-shirt was crisp and clean. And with the soot washed away, the skin at the centre of his chest appeared bright red and blistered.

Sawyer gave his head a short shake, felt his hair, inspected his clothes and then blinked at Zelie. "H-how did you do that?"

"Like I said, you weren't doing it properly," said Zelie, watching as one of the blue crystal shards dissolved from the wand. "And, you're welcome."

"I don't believe it," Sawyer huffed.

"Then I'll show you again."

She winked at Sawyer and raised the wand. Sawyer scrambled behind the beanstalk. But she was not aiming at him. She was pointing the wand at the gnomes. The smile on Bre's face dropped. Thurin closed his eyes in a tight squint and Dresden gritted his teeth.

Another star-filled cloud billowed from the end of the wand and blew away the pile of soot and dust that had dropped from Sawyer. The stars turned and swirled for a few moments and then vanished in a loud puff of mist. The gnomes stood agleam in their original comic poses, the messy blobs and stripes of Zelie's paint were gone, though the bumpy glue on Thurin's cheek remained. The corner of Dresden's mouth twitched happily. Thurin's eyebrows quivered and a glint shone in Bre's eye.

"Huh, should have tried that earlier," she said, as another three shards on the wand dissolved into blue dust. "Come on Sawyer, let's really test it. Show me where to find those pigs."

# CHAPTER EIGHT

## *Magic*

"Why does the wand work for you?" asked Sawyer, trotting to keep up with Zelie as she strode towards the pig shed.

"Let me guess. When you tried to cast the spell, you weren't thinking about what a nice thing you were doing for the pigs."

"No. But it would be nice for me. I don't want to clean them with my toothbrush. It's gross."

"And *that's* why you got a lightning bolt in the chest."

"Well that's just silly. The pigs don't care if they're clean or dirty. Even Auntie Ruth doesn't, really. She just makes me do it for punishment," Sawyer said. He pointed through the doorway at one of the pigs. "I think I singed old Agnes." The pig's bottom was black and some of the hairs were still smoking.

A thick stench wrinkled Zelie's nose as they entered the shed. "Cor, this cleaning job is a little overdue, don't you think?"

"Pigs always stink," Sawyer explained, "even after you wash them."

"What's that other smell? It's like… Is that bacon?"

"I think that's Agnes's burnt bottom." Agnes the pig oinked angrily at Sawyer. "I'm sorry girl, I was only trying to get you clean."

"Oh, this stink is horrible. Alright, let's do this."

She held up the wand. Sawyer covered his ears and

let out a frightened squeak. The wand sniffed sharply then sneezed out another cloud of stars. Zelie waved it from one side of the shed to the other and the pigs hopped into the air one at a time like a muddy Mexican wave. As each pig jolted back to the ground, the muck that encased it peeled off like a banana skin. The stars swirled and disappeared, leaving all the pigs clean, pink and oinking happily at each other. The scent of coconut and lemongrass filled the air.

Zelie gave a satisfied nod while Sawyer breathed in deeply through his nose. He looked at the pigs and huffed a small laugh of disbelief. "I don't think the pigs have ever been that clean." His gaze shifted to the wand where more blue shards were dissolving.

Zelie flipped the wand into the air, caught it in her other hand and handed it to Sawyer. "Give it a try. Just don't wish for anything *you* want."

Sawyer took the wand and rubbed his red chest through the hole in his white shirt. "I'm a little sore. Maybe later," Sawyer said. He pulled at his ear for a moment and then he held up the wand to examine it. "I don't get it. Why didn't you get struck by lightning like I did?" Sawyer asked, looking closely at one end of the wand as if something might be wrong with it.

"Because I didn't cast that spell for me."

"What? For the pigs, then?" Sawyer said.

"No. That spell was for *you*."

"Oh… right," said Sawyer, shooting her an uncomfortable glance. "Er, well, thanks."

"My pleasure."

Sawyer opened his mouth as if to speak but then thought better of it.

"What is it?" Zelie prompted.

Sawyer took a deep breath. "Do you think you could remove the curse from my Auntie?" he said in a hurry and then screwed up his face as if Zelie might throw something at him.

"A curse? Is that why her voice sounds like a bucket of nails in a blender?"

"I guess so. I don't really notice."

"And the freezing cold?" Zelie said.

"Yes, but that doesn't bother me either. I just want her to be nice to me."

"How do you know she was ever nice?" Zelie said and then immediately regretted it. Sawyer did not seem to mind.

"I've seen old pictures. There's one of her with me when I was a baby and she's smiling at me. I want that again. Please Zelie. She's the only family I've got."

"Well, I suppose I could try." Zelie's words left her mouth as a cloud of mist in the suddenly icy air. "Oh no."

"SAWYER!" screeched Auntie Ruth from somewhere outside.

Sawyer's face twisted with worry. He pointed towards the corner of the shed. "Qu—quick, hide. There's a worm tunnel under the hay bales."

"Worm tunnel?"

"Go," he hissed, pointing more aggressively.

As Zelie attempted to escape, her feet slipped on the frost that had already formed beneath her. On hands and knees she scrambled to get away, but slipped again and fell flat on her chest just as Auntie Ruth appeared in the doorway.

"Insect!" Ruth screeched with a mixture of disgust and delight. She wore rubber boots under a tattered and grimy skirt. A moth-eaten black cardigan hung loosely on her rounded shoulders and an oily tangle of dull hair fell over a scowling mouth so wrinkled and shrivelled that looked as if she had just been chewing a lemon.

But her eyes: somehow, they did not match the scathing voice and the angry scowl. Zelie's thoughts were cut short.

"I should have squashed you when I saw you crawling on the fence," she spat, striding towards Zelie. "Hold still, little bug. I'll fix you now."

Zelie struggled to regain her feet but failed to find any grip at all. This time she thudded hard on her back. Sawyer had the wand pointed at her. He shook his head and pointed it at Auntie Ruth, then back at Zelie, then back at Ruth. Auntie Ruth crunched over the frozen ground and the shadow of her boot shifted over Zelie's face. Sawyer took a shallow breath and closed his eyes.

A jumble of purple stars stampeded out of the wand and swept Zelie away like a feather in a storm. Intense pressure from all sides squeezed the air out of her lungs. She felt sure she would burst at any moment. But then the pressure released and she fell on warm moist ground, coughing. Inky blackness consumed her. The sweet smell of damp earth filled her nose.

A soft golden light cut through the dark: the glow from Zelie's hair. She pushed her stiff body off the curved ground and wiped the wet dirt from her cheek. She was inside a large tunnel under the ground. Muffled voices argued overhead. She guessed she was somewhere under the pig shed. But where the tunnel went or how far, she did not know because beyond the light of her hair, in both directions, she could see only darkness.

# CHAPTER NINE

## *Trembling Earth*

Zelie's body ached as if she had been squeezed through a garden hose. Sawyer must have finally worked out how to use the wand. Just in time too. A fraction of a second longer and Auntie Ruth would have fulfilled her promise to squash Zelie like a bug. Directly above Zelie, the underside of a row of hay bales formed a roof for the tunnel. She was underneath the pig shed. Smothered voices—Sawyer's defensive tone and Auntie Ruth's screech—were arguing above her.

She could not return the way she came, of course. But the tunnel seemed as if it should lead somewhere. There must be another way out, Zelie thought. But which way should she go? A quick verse of 'Eeny, Meeny, Miny, Moe' decided the direction and, with a deep breath of the warm moist air, she shuffled off in search of an exit.

Small water droplets swelled and fell from finger-like roots above her, landing at a lazy pace on her face and thudding into the wet earth around her. Larger tree roots meandered down the walls of the tunnel like thick veins. Water trickled down those too and into wavy rivulets on the tunnel floor. Beyond the cylinder of light that surrounded Zelie, there was only shadow.

The ground sloped downwards, at first, and then levelled out. It could have been her imagination, but Zelie felt as if the tunnel was becoming ever so slightly narrower as she moved along. What did Sawyer mean when he called this a worm tunnel? Earlier, the gnomes had said something about an earthworm. It sounded like nonsense at the time. What was it they said? The worm had absorbed some of the magic and burrowed into the ground by the beanstalk. Could this tunnel be the result?

By now she was certain the tunnel was shrinking. The worm must have been expanding as it made its way through the earth. And since the tunnel appeared to be getting gradually narrower, she must be heading towards the beanstalk where the worm was smallest. Her heartbeat quickened and her knees became shaky. She should have been glad to be going in the right direction. But with the walls closing in, it felt like the air was running out. How was she to escape? Surely, the tunnel would continue to contract as she neared the beanstalk. And what if the worm returned along the same path? Zelie shuddered and took a quick glance behind her. The tunnel was empty but for her own footprints leading out of the shadows. All the same, Zelie felt it was time to get above ground again.

She began to jog. But that just made the tunnel seem to shrink even more quickly. The splash and squelch of her shoes on the damp earth became steadily faster and the droplets dappled her face like gentle rain.

Suddenly, there was an almighty boom. The earth jolted violently and Zelie's feet evaporated beneath her, sending her into a twisted muddy sprawl. A sheet of rain fell from the roof of the tunnel, drenching her.

Spitting out the grit that had somehow made its way into her mouth and wiping the mud from her eyes, she wondered what on earth could rock the very ground like that. She was just unfolding herself from the floor of the tunnel when it happened again.

Boom. This time the ground seemed to rise up and

kick her in the chin. By the glow of her hair she could see cracks appearing in the walls of the tunnel. How long would it hold? Her heart pounded in her ears. Nursing her aching jaw, she sloshed to her feet and ran as fast as her legs would carry her.

Boom. Came the quake again. Her teeth chattered and her knees knocked together but, somehow, her feet stayed under her through the tremor. How far was it to the beanstalk? She had to be at least half way. Voices tittered above her between the explosions that seemed to be going off in the earth. Sawyer's muffled cry was moving overhead and Auntie Ruth's screech followed close behind. The tunnel had become so low now that Zelie had to stoop to avoid scraping her head on the ceiling.

Boom. Zelie was ready for the impact this time. This could not be an earthquake. It was too rhythmic. As absurd as it seemed, the most possible explanation was that the village was being bombed from the sky. But for what reason?

Suddenly, Zelie remembered. Sawyer and the gnomes had mentioned a giant. She had dismissed it as ridiculous at the time amongst the talk of unicorns and super earthworms. But the last few days had brought her a wand and animated gnomes and magic hair. Perhaps it was possible. Of all the things in her head now, strangely, it made the most sense. Yes. A giant—if there were such a thing—whose strides seemed to be travelling across the garden above, as if to intercept Sawyer and Auntie Ruth.

More urgent screeching rang out from above until it was silenced by the slam of a door.

"Eee—eye—oh—um!" came a deep muffled voice like a foghorn. It vibrated the ground. The roots poking into the tunnel quivered, dripping yet more dirty rain on

Zelie's mud-soaked clothes.

There was an almighty crack, then a brief bubbling noise like popcorn exploding under the lid of a saucepan. And then the sound of tyres skidding to a halt. It was only later that Zelie understood this last noise to be Ruth shrieking in terror. The tunnel began to slope upwards again, levelling out under a series of wooden boards. A horse joined the chorus of mayhem overhead with a series of urgent neighs and the wooden clop of its hooves.

The shake of another booming footstep rattled Zelie's bones and made the wooden boards above her clatter and rain dust. To her horror, suddenly the tunnel ahead collapsed, blocking her path. The horse whinnied longer and louder and clomped its feet on the floor of what Zelie now realised was the stable. She pressed upwards on the wooden planks, desperate to escape. The first plank would not budge. But to her relief, the second one lifted easily and pushed over to one side, bringing dust and straw down on her head along with a chilling breeze.

A creak, wooden—like the fence, but louder— reached her ears. It had to be the beanstalk.

The loop of a nearby tree root served as a foothold and, with all her strength, Zelie hefted her water-soaked body out of the tunnel, landing on the floor of the stable with a loud squelch.

The air was freezing on her wet clothes and hair. The horse clopped its hooves inches from her head and she rolled onto her feet to get out of the way. Finally safe from the collapsing tunnel, she breathed a sigh of relief.

The beanstalk continued to creak. The giant must be climbing it, she thought. Zelie's comfort at being free of the tunnel lasted two seconds before it gave way to a feeling of desperate curiosity. How big was the giant? What did it look like? What had it done with Auntie Ruth to make her scream like that?

The creaking was becoming softer as the giant climbed higher. Zelie's opportunity to see him was dwindling with every second.

The horse nuzzled her with its nose, puffing warm moist clouds of tickling breath into her neck. "Not now, Horsey," she said.

After a brief scan around the stable, she found the only door and ran to it. She lifted the latch, but something heavy was resting against the outside, jamming the door closed. Zelie took a step back and kicked with all her strength. But the door scraped forwards only a fraction of its full arc and then teased her with a juddering giggle.

Zelie had to see. She just had to. So with her eyes tightly closed, she thrust her head through the small gap, almost stripping off her ears. A painful contortion gave her a strained glimpse of the dusk sky just as the shadow of a huge creature climbed up inside the cloud with a final faint wooden creak. The whole beanstalk was bowing in the shape of a banana from the ground to the cloud under the giant's immense weight until, a moment later, it straightened; presumably as the giant stepped off onto some platform in the sky.

Zelie's body went limp with disappointment. Besmeared with mud, wet through to her skin and sandwiched diagonally in the doorway of a stable, her whole body was filled with a cold ache. Her gaze drooped. Bathed in the orange glow from her hair, she saw what had kept the door from opening. A broken mess of stones and mortar seemed to have been swept up against the stable wall. Where had it come from? Shattered glass and bricks were strewn across the ground as far as the light would reach.

With a good deal of grunting, Zelie managed to shift the largest of the stones and free herself from the doorframe. As she stepped towards the beanstalk, inspecting the mess, she saw that the house was in ruin. One of its walls had been torn completely away and half of the roof was missing. Inside the yawning cavern of broken stones were the remains of the kitchen where a large pot of overflowing grey liquid was still bubbling on the stove.

The garden was almost unrecognisable from the giant's pounding of it. Zelie felt as if she had been placed into a shrunken world, brutalised by a belligerent child. The ground looked like a layer of green clay, punched and squashed into craters and mounds, peppered with rubble and sprinkled with scrunched up beanstalk leaves. The leaf pile had been pushed to one side to reveal the edge of an enormous tree stump. It was so big that you could park a car on the edge that was showing. The rest of the stump was still hidden under the remaining leaves. The chimney was on its side, propped up on one of the mounds of squashed grass. Broken pieces of crockery, in somehow familiar colours of faded green and yellow, lay scattered around it.

Out of the shadows, Thurin and Dresden moped into the garden and began shifting saucepans and cupboard doors and kicking away bricks. Their blue and red hats bobbed down and up, down and up as they collected some things and threw others away.

Dresden noticed her watching and gave a stuttered sniff. Thurin stopped and gazed at Zelie through teary eyes. In their tiny hands they had collected pieces of clay, but only those that were coloured in yellow and green. A lump expanded in Zelie's throat.

"It's Bre," croaked Dresden.

"What are we going to do?" Thurin added with a wavering voice.

Zelie had a sinking feeling that this was well beyond her repair skills to mend. "I know, we'll use the wand," she suggested.

The gnomes exchanged a glance, looked down at the pile of pieces that used to be Bre and shook their heads, solemnly.

"What is it? Did the giant take it? What did he look like?"

The gnomes went about their work without a word. 'Speechless' was not a description Zelie had ever expected to apply to the gnomes. But perhaps they did not see what happened? Perhaps they did not care about the giant? Perhaps they were simply too upset about Bre to speak?

Sawyer emerged from the shadows. "The giant—" he started, then fell silent.

"Oh there you are," said Zelie. "Are you alright?"

Sawyer's face was pale and his eyes were wide with fright. "The giant took Auntie," he gushed, as if he had been holding back the words: as if saying them made it real.

Zelie had a moment of internal celebration that she was gone. She probably got what she deserved, she thought. Sawyer saw her fleeting delight and looked through her with a blank stare. A fist of guilt clenched inside Zelie's stomach. She was about to apologise when Sawyer lurched forward as if he had been whipped from behind. He leaped over the rubble and dented ground and straight past Zelie and began pushing the leaves back into a heap over the enormous stump.

"What are you doing?" Zelie said.

"The stump," he said, meekly. "It's not allowed to be seen. Auntie says so. I'm supposed to keep it covered or I get in trouble."

Zelie ran to him and took hold of his hands. "Stop Sawyer. Look around."

Sawyer surveyed the garden and sighed. "She's the only family I've got."

Zelie frowned and gave him a brief hug.

"How am I going to get her back?" asked Sawyer.

Zelie could not understand why, but it was clear that Sawyer desperately wanted his Auntie. "Do you have the wand?" asked Zelie. She had no idea whether the wand was capable of transporting Ruth back, but there was nothing to lose in trying.

"The giant took it."

Zelie frowned again and then glanced over at the gnomes who were still glumly picking the embedded pieces of Bre out of the ground. They did not even seem to mind that Sawyer was around any more.

"The gnomes might know what to do," Zelie suggested. "Gnomes, do you have any ideas?"

Thurin and Dresden stopped and looked up at her forlornly. Had they lost the power of speech? Was the magic from the bean wearing off? Then it struck Zelie that they had shared responsibility for speaking in every conversation so far.

"Oh, I understand now," Zelie exclaimed. "It's Bre's turn to speak."

The gnomes nodded sadly.

"OK, let me give you a hand to pick up her pieces."

The ground was more like an obstacle course than a garden with all the pits and mounds in it. As Zelie took the safest path she could to reach the gnomes, she stepped down inside one of the craters. It was shaped like a stretched oblong with five smaller pits at one end.

The pits diminished in size from right to left, as if they were made by a huge set of toes.

"Gosh, I'm inside a giant's footprint aren't I?" she exclaimed.

The gnomes said nothing and stared only briefly before returning to their task.

Zelie sighed. "Don't be sad you two. If we work together, I'm sure we can glue her back together," she said, trying to ignore Thurin rubbing at his lumpy cheek. "We'll just have to make sure we have all the pieces."

Dresden pointed at the base of the chimney under which a few green pieces of Bre were trapped.

"Yes, I see them. We need that chimney out of the way, don't we?" Zelie was about to ask Sawyer to help her roll the chimney when there was a faint tinkle in her ears.

"Of course!" she said excitedly, realising the source of the sound. "Right. Stand back everyone. I don't know exactly how well this will work. A little further—that's it. Now, hair," she said loudly, "Get this chimney out of the way."

Immediately, her scalp tightened. A number of thick blond tendrils unfurled over her shoulder and slithered under the chimney. With a loud chime and a sharp jerk, the column of bricks flew into the air as if it were as light as polystyrene. It tumbled through the air, scraped past the lower beanstalk leaves and landed directly on the fence, crumpling one of the panels right to the ground with a loud crunch. Broken planks and wire-wrapped branches spilled into the garden and out to the alley.

"Sweet blue blazes!" a deep voice exclaimed. "Now it's raining chimneys," Jack's sheepskin hat appeared sideways through the gap made by the flattened fence panel.

"Jack!" chirped Zelie.

"Squirrel. If it weren't for that glowing head of yours, I'd have never recognised you under that layer of filth." He stepped out of the dark laneway, past the remains of the chimney and ran his gaze over the destruction before him. "So this is what you call being careful, is it?" he said, lifting his chin at Zelie. "What are you doing here?"

"I came to fix the gnomes," Zelie said.

"And a fine job you're doing of that," Jack said, nodding at the pile of terracotta pieces that Thurin and Dresden had assembled. He had not seemed to register that the gnomes had come to life.

"What are *you* doing here?" Zelie said, trying to deflect his attention.

"I spotted Max and thought I'd come and talk some sense into him." He stepped over an upside down ceiling fan. "Good thing I didn't rush. If I had arrived a moment earlier, I might have been underneath that bit of fence."

"Who's Max?" Zelie said.

"The big guy with a fondness for beanstalks," Jack said. "I expect you call him *the giant.*"

"So why do you call him Max?"

"That's his name."

"Well, how would you know that?"

Jack sighed and shook his head. "Keeping secrets is like trying to hold water in your hands; no matter how tightly you hold your fingers, eventually it leaks through. I suppose there's no harm in talking about it now is there? The damage is done, as they say." He kicked a piece of rubble into one of the huge footprints. "The truth is, Max wasn't always a giant. He was just a little boy."

"So how did he become a giant?"

"Well to explain that, I'd have to say the 'm' word."

"You mean, magic?" Zelie said, widening her eyes and speaking a little more loudly than she needed to.

Jack rolled his eyes and nodded.

"You're still not telling me something," observed Zelie.

Jack shook his head. "You know me too well, Squirrel."

"So what is it then?" Zelie demanded.

"Well, I suppose you would say the giant is—" He trailed off as if he had changed his mind. Then he sighed and nodded decisively. "The giant is my brother."

# CHAPTER TEN

## *Spilled Beans*

Zelie frowned at Jack. "What do you mean *the giant is your brother?*" The words escaped her much louder than she intended. But Jack was accustomed to Zelie's outbursts.

"I mean, he's mio fratello, me bro, or, as Max used to say when he was a baby: me Ba-Bah" Jack said, smiling and shaking his head nostalgically. Then he gave a lop-sided nod and said: "but now, sadly, he's a large smelly hairy thing that people call a giant. "

Zelie had so many questions; she did not know where to start.

Jack put his hands on his hips and nodded at the partially exposed stump. "I see you've discovered the other beanstalk."

"Other beanstalk?" Zelie asked, feeling lightheaded.

"Not my neatest work but I was only about thirteen when I chopped it down. I was strong as an ox and just as bright. If it wasn't for Ruth's quick thinking, Max would have fallen to his death."

"Oh, I have to sit down," said Zelie.

"Oh how rude of me," Jack said, turning to Sawyer. "I'm Jack. I used to live in this very house."

"The giant took my Auntie," Sawyer said to Jack, absently.

"I see," Jack said. "I am sorry. He's probably acting under some very old order."

"His name is Sawyer," Zelie said, bobbing her head

towards the boy when he failed to give his name.

"*This* is young *Sawyer*?" Jack said, surprised. "My, how you've grown." Then his face lit up and pointed to the blisters on Sawyer's chest. "You've got a wand? Well bless your little cotton socks. Where is it?"

Sawyer's expression went from shock to disappointment. "Auntie had it," looking towards the sky.

Jack tutted. "No matter. No matter at all. This is still the best news in a decade. All we have to do is get it back find someone who knows how to use it and we can say good bye to this cloud for the very last time. We could ask your mother, Squirrel."

"My mother?" Zelie shrieked.

"No, you're right. She was better with concoctions than wands."

"What?" Zelie said, even louder.

"It was Ruth who was the whizz with the wand," Jack said, emphatically.

Zelie's surprise turned to confusion.

"What is it Squirrel? You look like you've swallowed a fork."

"Auntie Ruth? Good at making unselfish spells?"

"Oh, she hasn't always been the cold and heartless fence builder that you think you know," explained Jack. "She's lovely. But where's my head? Her curse will put a stop to any good deeds, won't it? We'll have to find someone else."

"I know how to use it now," announced Sawyer, gesturing at Zelie as if the fact that she was standing there caked in mud was proof of his abilities. "And I know a spell that ends curses. I got it for Auntie but I guess it would work on the cloud as well."

Jack frowned and spoke quietly. "Where would you have learned a spell like that?"

"The witch," Sawyer said, pointing to the clouds.

"Here we go again," Zelie said with a groan. She expected Jack to tell Sawyer not to be so silly. But, if anything, he encouraged more madness.

"What witch?" Jack said, concerned.

"*The* witch," Sawyer said. "The one that put the curse on Auntie. Her name is, er—Madelene."

Jack gasped. "Where did you hear that name, Sawyer," he said, becoming more serious than Zelie had ever seen.

"At the market," Sawyer said, looking as if he wanted to take his words back.

"Keep going," Jack said, quietly, as he crouched into a squat and pressed a hand over his mouth.

"Alright," Jack said and cleared his throat. "I was only there to sell our old cow. I could tell she wasn't a merchant from the way she was dressed. She didn't even have any money. But she really wanted the cow. She asked me what I wanted most in the world. I said I wanted my Auntie to be as kind as she looks in all the old photographs. Then she tried to get me to sell the cow for some beans. I didn't believe they were magic until she used one of them to do this." Sawyer held up his right hand and wiggled his fingers. It took Zelie a moment to register that the hand had two thumbs—one on each side. How had she not noticed it before?

"I might have fainted for a little while," Sawyer said, looking ashamed. "When I woke up, she was using some sort of magic so that nobody could see or hear us. I thought she was reading my mind because she called me by my name and she already knew that Auntie had a wand. I wanted to get out of there as quickly as I could so I gave her the cow for the beans and she taught me the spell. I thought that was going to be it. But she wouldn't let me leave until I bowed and said her name:

Queen Madelene. I only remember because the words rhyme: Madelene and Queen, you know?"

Jack washed his face hard with his hands and groaned.

"She also said I had to tell Auntie that I sold the cow for some beans," said Sawyer.

"Of course she did," said Jack, with an exaggerated head movement. "To cause a fight so that Ruth would throw out the beans," Jack said with a wave at the beanstalk. "That's exactly how she gets you." He clenched his fists and yelled: "blast that scheming witch! How did she survive? And where's she been hiding for the last ten years?"

"Jack!" exclaimed Zelie, angrily. "You don't really believe all that do you?"

"Look at his thumbs, Squirrel. That's exactly the kind of stunt the witch uses. Blast!" he said again and stamped his foot. "Madelene, back from the dead. When Ruth cast her into the sea with that wand, I was sure she was pickled for good." He stood quickly, a look of urgency on his face. "We've got to get out of here. Max isn't acting under old orders at all, it's that damn witch." He cast a glance up the beanstalk. "It's just gone nightfall. If it's anything like last time, Max will be back down again very soon with fresh orders. No one is safe from him. Not even me."

Zelie was still struggling to understand how this was all possible. But if the giant could destroy the garden the way he had, she did not want to be around if he was coming back down. She scooped up the pieces of Bre and dropped them into her back pack. "Hide somewhere safe," she told the other gnomes. "I'll come back for you later."

The gnomes nodded solemnly.

Jack led Zelie and Sawyer past what remained of the

chimney and through the gap in the fence.

"Freeze!" ordered a man who had a moustache so bushy that it hung over his mouth. He was about Jack's age and was wearing a police uniform.

"Good," encouraged an older man who was standing a little further behind him wearing a matching outfit. "Excellent tone of voice. Good authority." As he spoke, he ticked boxes on some kind of form on a clipboard.

"You're all under arrest for suspected use of magic," said the younger policeman, tilting his chin to the beanstalk and gesturing to the top of Zelie's head.

"By authority of?" prompted the older man.

"By authority of the Right Honourable Lord Mayor Douglas Andrews under section 6 of the Emerson Penal Code."

"Excellent. Now the badge," said the older man.

The younger man flipped open a leather wallet to reveal a silver police badge, which Jack immediately swatted to the ground with his hand.

"We don't have time for this Neville," Jack said. "I've just found out the witch is still alive."

The policemen looked shocked. They shot an anxious glance at Sawyer and Zelie as if they should not have been exposed to the word 'witch'. The older man consulted his clipboard as if looking for guidance about what to do in this sort of situation.

The younger one puffed out a breath, making his moustache lift up and dance about. "You can't say that sort of thing, Jack," he said, softly. "Er, I mean, you will cease speaking on that illegal subject matter immediately, Sir," he said, deepening his voice again. "Unless you want me to add 'spreading stories about mystical arts' to your charges."

"Add whatever you like Neville. We've got to make

ourselves scarce, pronto!"

"Sir," continued Neville in his authoritative voice. "I shall now escort you and your companions to the police vehicle in which you will be taken to the station for processing."

"Good recovery," said the older man, looking relieved and scribbling a note on his form. "Full marks so far."

"This is Madelene's doing," said Jack. "It's the same as last time. I think you ought to send Barry and Noodles down here to evacuate the terrace houses. She'll be sending Max down to cause trouble next. And then we had all better brace ourselves. Who knows what new spells she has been conjuring up in the last decade."

The officers gasped and Neville held up his hand in front of Jack's mouth as if trying to hold back the words.

"Protocol allows the use of a gag in this scenario," whispered the older man.

Neville fumbled to unhook something at his waist making the contents of his belt jingle. But Zelie was certain she heard a sound that could not possibly have come from the officer's duty belt.

"Did you hear that?" she said.

"Every word," said the older officer. "He'll be in big trouble for this, Miss. That sort of language is strictly forbidden."

"No not that. Just listen."

And that's when Zelie heard it clearly. High in the sky, a distant *creak* cut through the still night.

# CHAPTER ELEVEN

## *Run!*

"You heard that, right?" Zelie said, wide eyed. "That creaking sound."

The police officers looked stunned. The beanstalk began to bend and gave off an agonised groan under a massive weight. The older policeman gave a brief glance at his clip board and then tossed it clattering to the ground before fleeing towards the police car at the end of the laneway.

"We'll just call this a warning then," said Neville and chased after the older man. They were surprisingly nimble despite their pudgy physiques.

"It's Max!" shouted Jack. "He'll be under Madelene's order. We've got to get out of sight."

Creak went the beanstalk again.

Jack grabbed Zelie's hand and pulled her into a run. "Come on Sawyer, knees up."

Zelie's backpack slipped off her shoulder too quickly for her to grab it. She turned to see it roll on the ground before it was engulfed in the shadows beyond the light of her hair.

It should have been some comfort to be able to see every bump and crack in the path by the glow from her head. But all Zelie could think about was how she must look to the giant. What an easy target she made: like a firefly without wings.

Creak.

She needed to be out of sight, and quickly. Then it

occurred to her. Her hair had obeyed other orders. It was worth a try, at least.

"Hair, go dark?" she said, as if it were a question.

In an instant, the black of the night consumed the laneway. It was as if someone had blown out a candle in a windowless room. Zelie felt blind but knew she must continue, although now she was as unsure of each stride as a baby learning to walk.

The police were quite a way ahead by now. They flicked on their torches and waved them around as they sprinted for safety. It did not help to reveal the bumps and other obstacles in the path, but at least it gave Zelie a direction to run.

Creak!

Jack stumbled over some obstacle and released Zelie's hand. There was a dull thud as he hit the ground.

"Don't wait for me. Keep going!" Jack's strained voice urged her.

The earth shook as the giant's feet hit the ground, turning Zelie's legs to jelly. She saw Sawyer's shadowy silhouette collapse beside her. But unlike Zelie who scuffed her hands and scraped the skin from one knee, he rolled and was back on his feet in an instant. Before she realised what had happened, his cold hand was already heaving her off the ground.

"Let's go," puffed Sawyer.

The police car screeched away leaving nothing but a cloud of exhaust smoke that shone red until the rear lights of the car disappeared leaving Zelie, Jack and Sawyer hopelessly alone in the dark.

"We're not through yet. Run like your feet are afire," Jack shouted as he sprinted past.

"FEE—FI—FO—FUM," bellowed a deep voice. The ground let out a brief crumbling growl under the weight of the giant. An almighty crash signalled the demise of another fence panel. Splinters of wood zipped past Zelie's ears while others lodged in her hair. Then the ground shook as the giant took a first step towards them. Zelie staggered and bit down hard as the ground trembled.

Another step crunched down, so near this time that the wind from the descending foot gusted hair into her face. They could not keep this up. In two or three steps, the giant would be on top of them. But there was a rhythm to the footsteps, just as there had been in the worm tunnel. And Zelie had an idea.

"Jump just before the next quake!" she shouted.

"What?" screamed Sawyer over the rumble of breaking ground.

"Jump, now!"

They leapt into the air like a pair of gazelles. The giant's foot pounded the earth. But Sawyer and Zelie sailed above the vibrating path and past a staggering Jack. They landed smoothly and charged towards the street.

"Again!" squealed Zelie. "3-2-1-Jump!" Up into the air, they bounded as the world shook beneath them. It was working.

At the corner, Zelie hurried a glance back down the laneway. Jack was just visible in the light shining from a nearby streetlight. He had taken to the same running-leaping pattern. And behind him, eclipsing the beanstalk, the giant's mountainous shadow loped side to side towards them.

"Left," yelled Jack, waving them to go on.

The streetlights shone down on the road: bright circles between dark spaces. In and out of the light they ran. As they jumped the quaking earth, cracks streaked across the illuminated pavement, reaching underneath them like a rampant thicket. Parked cars hopped at each foot strike and then nodded, as if approving of their progress. They were gaining a lot of ground now.

Zelie glanced back over her shoulder. Behind Jack, a gigantic knee appeared out of the night's dark abyss into the downward-facing beam of the streetlight. A colossal foot swung forwards into view and slammed into the road, shattering its surface. Distracted by the sight, Zelie mistimed her jump. The shockwave hit, pulling her hand out of Sawyer's grasp and sending her skidding on her shoulder.

"On your feet, Squirrel," Jack chirped, grabbing Zelie's elbow and pulling her arm so hard that she left the ground. "Shake a leg."

Zelie glanced back again. The giant's foot had peeled off the road and was airborne towards her. Chunks of concrete and earth fell from the underfoot as it lifted from its massive imprint. Jack gave another yank on Zelie's arm. "Quickly now. No time for sight seeing."

With a swift dip, he scooped up a rock from the pavement and hurled it ahead. It disappeared into the black between the lights then smashed into the globe right outside his house. Glass and sparks rained down on Sawyer who groaned and crumpled to the ground as the fireworks fell all around him.

"Up you hop, Sawyer. It's this way," Jack yelled as he crunched past over the broken glass, kicked open the gate and ran up the garden path. "No need to wipe your feet," he jested, dragging Zelie up the steps and bursting through the front door.

Jack's hand let go of hers and suddenly she was alone inside his house. Jack was running back through the shadows for Sawyer. The dim glow through the front doorway was the only light. Zelie had no idea which way to go. The air was thick with powdery dust. Something made of glass smashed on the floor in a nearby room.

The pound of the giant's next footstep made a nearby wall split with a deafening crack and Zelie's legs could not hold her. Only Inches from hitting the floor, Jack scooped Zelie onto her feet and barrelled her forwards, side-by-side with Sawyer whose shadowy arms were flailing blindly in front of him. The wooden patter of their feet on the floorboards was a drumroll. Ceiling grit rained on her face and hissed on the floor. The taste of old paint and plaster was in her mouth. Spluttering, she reached out into the darkness for a wall into which she was surely going to collide. But somehow, Jack seemed to know exactly where they were in the house. His clamp-like grip heaved Zelie to a stop and he pushed past roughly, knocking her into the wall.

The house shook and rattled as the giant stomped one humongous step closer. A nearby table saved Zelie from falling to the floor, while somewhere nearby a door squeaked open. There was the sound of Sawyer yelping followed by a thud. Then Jack's iron grip took Zelie by the shoulder and steered her onwards. But there was no ground to meet her foot and she fell forwards. A few moments of terrifying weightlessness later, she landed flat on her front, expelling a hoarse grunt as the breath disappeared from her lungs. Jack landed beside her and the door above them squeaked and thumped shut. They must be in the basement, she thought.

"Not a sound or he'll know where to find us," whispered Jack. The giant's footsteps were like explosions and Zelie felt like her bones might shatter. She gritted her teeth at each earth-crumbling footfall.

There was an agonising silence. Then the rushing of wind as the giant took a breath. "I smell the blood of an

Englishman!" bellowed the giant, shaking Zelie like a leaf.

A moment later there was a scraping noise, like metal grinding over rock. It began above them and shifted downward until it seemed to be coming at them from everywhere. Then the whole room shifted violently to one side and upwards. Glass and crockery smashed in the rooms above. The house snapped and cracked and Zelie had a giddy, sick feeling. The room itself seemed to be moving up and rotating sideways. Zelie slid against the wall, followed by Sawyer. Piercing pain ran through her chest as his knee connected with her ribs. Paint tins and various tools clattered and clanged dangerously close to her head. The whole house creaked and shuddered as if it were about to splinter apart at any moment.

"Salt in my sugar bowl," hissed Jack. "He's lifted the whole house up. Squirrel, flick the switch on that fancy noggin will you? We'll solve this pickle yet."

"Hair, alight," she called.

An orange glow filled the room and Zelie found herself on a mattress next to Sawyer. But since the whole house had been tipped on its side, she was actually lying on the wall of the basement. Jack's normally calm expression was twisted with worry. "Let's get you two sorted. Lie close now, side-by-side. Hurry—that's it." He fought to keep his balance as the house jerked and jolted. He rolled Sawyer and Zelie in the mattress. "Now Squirrel. Let's see what you can do to keep these sides together," he prompted with encouraging eyes.

"What about you?" she asked, desperately.

"Never mind that. We have a tick of the clock at most. Do it now before it's too late!" he yelled.

"Hair, wrap around the mattress," she called out,

awkwardly. It sounded like a strange command. But it worked.

Glowing strands spiralled in front of Zelie's face. The last she saw was Jack nodding in approval. A moment later, she was inside a cocoon of glowing hair.

The giant gave a heaving grunt from outside and the world shifted powerfully sideways. She hit the opposite wall with crushing force and blacked out.

# CHAPTER TWELVE

## *Out of the Ruins*

Zelie's grazed shoulder shrieked with pain, shocking her awake. The smell of antiseptic invaded her nose and pierced her behind the eyes, making them water.

"Ow! That hurts," she hissed, propping herself up on her elbows and peering for the source of the pain with one squinted eye. Beth was kneeling by her side with a steaming pink cotton ball in her fingers. "Mum! What are you doing?"

"Oh goodness, Darling, I'm so glad you're awake," said Beth. "You've been unconscious since we found you. My sweet girl, if your love of adventure is not the death of you, it will be of me. But bless my spectacles, if your hair hasn't ever looked so lovely."

Zelie was lying on the mattress from Jack's basement. But now it was morning and she was in the town park near the seaside. The park area looked as if it had exploded. Sawyer was lying on a nearby park bench nursing a grazed elbow. His heavy mop of hair was messy and matted to one side. Little white strips held together a cut on his forehead and one of his cheeks was bruised. He gave Zelie a wincing wave.

All around them were scattered bricks, tiles, concrete, plaster, books, pieces of broken furniture along with tree branches and leaves. Some of the items were half embedded in the ground, angled away from the sea. Others lay loose. Deep gouges scarred the earth where rubble had skidded, peeling back sheets of moss to uncover beds of dark earth, before finding a place to rest.

"Is all this from Jack's house?" asked Zelie, incredulously.

"Can you believe it?" Beth pointed the cotton ball at the tattered remains of a tiled roof poking from the water. "Jack built that house with his own hands. Now look at it. Poor man. Though I suppose that's the least of his worries."

Jack's place was a good five minute walk from the park. The fact that the giant had managed to tear the house from the ground was astonishing. But then he had sent it all that way through the air with a swing of his arm?

Beth resumed her dabbing of Zelie's painful shoulder wound. "Praise the saints for whatever miracle saved you. If only poor Jack had your good fortune. I do hope he will be all right." The words hit Zelie like ice water.

"Poor Jack? What do you mean? Where is he?" she blurted, grabbing the cotton ball out of Beth's hand.

Beth tilted her head and turned a worried glance to the distance. Zelie twisted painfully to see. Jack's legs were jutting, unmoving, from the open doors of an ambulance. Her stomach pulled into a tight knot.

"He hasn't woken up," said Beth. "The paramedics… It doesn't look good."

Zelie pried her aching body off the ground and walked stiffly towards the ambulance.

"What are you doing?" Beth cried after her. "Now wait a minute. I haven't finished swabbing the gravel out of that shoulder."

"I can't now, Mum. I've got to see him."

As Zelie hobbled towards Jack, Sawyer joined her side. He opened his mouth to talk but must have thought better of it. Instead, he quickened his pace and arrived at the ambulance a moment before Zelie. His mouth dropped open in horror as he saw inside. The knot in Zelie's stomach tightened.

Jack lay deathly still on a gurney. Every inch of this head was covered in medical dressings with only enough space between the bandages on his face for an oxygen mask. Plastic tubes and electrical leads ran from his chest and arms to a machine that emitted a slow beep. More bandages were wound around one of his arms. Blood had soaked through in patches and the skin that was visible appeared pale and sickly. Heat rose in Zelie's chest and an ache grew thick in her throat. This was her fault. If she had not dropped the beans, then perhaps the beanstalk would not have grown. Then none of this would have happened.

Jack had done everything he could to keep her from harm. He had wrapped her in the mattress. And she left him with nothing. How could she? Why did she? She felt as witless as that idiot giant.

Beth's hand stroked her arm and Zelie jumped. "You mustn't blame yourself, sweetheart," Beth said, as if reading her mind. "This is the giant's doing."

"And the witch," added Sawyer.

"Pssht! Now, now. We mustn't talk about such things," Beth scolded.

"She's alive," Zelie said. "The giant is under her control. Right Sawyer?"

Sawyer nodded. "And she's got my Auntie."

"And her wand," Zelie said.

Beth seemed to deflate and her stare drifted to the ground. "Not this again."

"Jack said you've used magic before," Zelie said.

"Shhh," Beth hissed, glancing around to see if anyone might have heard. "Must you be so loud?"

"Oh my gosh. So it is true?" Zelie said more quietly. "Well, couldn't you cast a spell or something to help Jack? Please Mum. You know he would do anything for us."

"Now just a minute, I-" Beth started.

"You've got to," Zelie interrupted. "Just once. Please?"

"Zelie, Dear! Quiet for a moment. Let me think." Beth stared at the ground with a furrowed brow while Zelie jiggled her knees impatiently. "There is only a small chance," Beth sighed, rummaging inside her handbag and pulling out a small purple bottle with white polkadots. "I saved the remaining water from the basin. That silent flash," she said, lowering her voice to a whisper. "It often happens when charms become activated. It's not always the case, but if there was any magic in that bean-"

"I'll have that bottle please," Zelie said into the air. She had barely finished speaking when a lock of her hair lashed the polkadot bottle from Beth's hands and placed it in her own. "What do you think now?"

"Goodness!" said Beth, wide eyed and scanning the area again. "You must be more discreet, dear. Just because another beanstalk has miraculously popped up doesn't mean you won't be arrested for using magic." She stroked Zelie's hair, which emitted a chime. "But, my oh my, what a special gift."

"So you'll help him?" Zelie asked, handing back the bottle. Beth eyed it for a moment then nodded decisively.

"Alright dear, just this once, but you must stand back, both of you. He's likely to twitch. And I think if I just pour the concoction where he's hurt, like here and here—watch out!"

Jack's body thrashed about wildly and then went

still again. The machine beeped erratically—as if it was delivering Morse code—then sped up to a frantic pace before returning to its lethargic rhythm.

"What are you doing there?" said a paramedic, gruffly. He was pushing an old lady in a wheelchair with a gash on her lower leg.

Beth jumped at the sound of his voice and made a poor attempt to hide the bottle behind her back.

"Is that a concoction?" gasped the paramedic. "Get that away from my patient."

He wheeled the old lady to the curb, stepped up inside the ambulance and sat beside the gurney. He felt Jack's pulse and performed various other examinations on him. "Whatever you've done has made him worse," said the paramedic. "I'll have to report this. You must know it's against the law to use enchantments." He was clearly exasperated and turned his back to twist dials and press coloured buttons on the machine connected to Jack.

With a reluctant look, Zelie's mother tipped the polkadot bottle over her cupped hand and whispered something close to the spout. The liquid poured out of the bottle but instead of welling in her hand, it hovered in a sphere a few inches above it. As Beth continued to whisper, the liquid swirled in the air and changed from clear to bright pink. Beth's lips were still moving when she extended her arm, casting the pink ball at the paramedic just as he turned to face them. The liquid expanded into a haze, which spun around the paramedic's head. Then it poured into his eyes and ears. His hair fluttered and his body stiffened at first, then he went limp and slumped against the inside wall of the ambulance. Then as if snapping out of a daze, he rubbed his eyes, shook his head and sat forward. He examined Jack as if for the first time, checked the machine, twisted another dial and tutted.

Then he stood quickly and made to get out of the ambulance, almost bowling Zelie over in the process. "Oh sorry about that Miss. Oh, and Ma'am, Sir. I beg your pardon. I didn't know you were all standing there. I must have been in my own little world. Are you friends of this man?"

"Er, yes," Zelie said quietly, after a short pause. Did he not remember?

"Well, you can follow me to the hospital if you like. But I must go immediately—oh, look here's another one," he said, as if the lady in the wheelchair had arrived beside the ambulance on her own. "Hello Madam. Are you in need of aid for that gash on your leg?"

The lady looked at Zelie's mother, then down at the polkadot bottle. She shook her head frantically at the paramedic and pulled her skirt down over the wound.

"Don't mind me, Sonny. That man needs you more than I do." And with an imploring nod at Zelie's mother, she swivelled the wheelchair and rolled away in a hurry.

Zelie's mother waited until the ambulance disappeared in a cacophony of sirens and flashing lights. "You see, my love, magic has a strange dark power. I mustn't use it any more. I ought not to have used it in the first place."

"Did the magic really make him worse than he was before?" Zelie asked.

"I don't know—I don't know. Oh dear. What I was thinking?"

"Well can't you just undo it? Zelie suggested.

"It can be done, Sweetheart, but only by someone with a wand," Beth said.

Zelie felt a strange sensation as if the air had shivered. "Attention!" came an echoing voice from the sky.

"That's Madelene's voice," Sawyer gasped.

"People of Emerson. This is your queen," the voice continued as if it were on loudspeaker. "Though I am thoroughly displeased with the traitorous and undignified events of the past, I am prepared to forgive them if you will now conform to my will."

Zelie could recognise that Madelene was speaking in English but none of it made any real sense to her. It sounded as if she was trying to impress everyone with big words.

"A queen must have royal subjects," the voice went on. "The young have not been imbued with the irreversibly foul habits common to older peasants. With focus and training, some of them will develop regal standards of service. Therefore, all children aged five years and under are to be deposited at the base of the beanstalk by this time of the day tomorrow. They will be absorbed into the service of the crown. Mayor Andrews, I'm sure, will help to facilitate my orders. If any person fails to recognise the authority of the royal house, I will destroy every one of yours. That is all."

The air shivered again and the voice was gone. "Oh dear," said Beth.

"Did you understand what she was saying?" Zelie asked Beth.

"She wants to take the children as slaves," explained Beth.

"She also said something about destroying the village, didn't she?" asked Sawyer.

"If we don't do as she commands, yes," Beth said. "I expect she will send down the giant again. Oh, she is such a beastly woman."

"Someone should stand up to her," suggested Sawyer.

Zelie gave him a bemused look but then nodded in agreement. Someone should, probably not Sawyer though.

"No," Beth said, shaking her head sadly. "No, it would be very unwise to face her directly. She is too powerful."

"I'm going to go up there," decided Zelie.

Beth looked shocked.

"Just to get the wand," Zelie explained. "Then we can undo whatever spells she throws at us and help Jack get better."

"And get my Auntie?" Sawyer added.

"This is not the time for adventures, Zelie."

"There might not be another time, *Mother*."

"Please don't go up there on your own." Beth's voice cracked and her eyes began to glisten with tears. "I know there's no use in telling you that you can't because you will do it anyway. But I've already lost a loved one to the witch. I can't bear the thought of—" She pressed her hands over her mouth and shook her head.

"I'll go with her," Sawyer offered. For a moment, Zelie looked at him, confused. "I want to get my Auntie back anyway. And I really don't want to face that witch." Zelie had thought as much. "I know how dangerous she is. And the giant." Sawyer's voice trailed off as if he was regretting his suggestion already. But to Zelie's surprise, Beth looked relieved.

"Sawyer's Auntie can end the curse," Zelie added, sensing Sawyer was about to back out right when Zelie was on the verge of winning Beth's permission. "Then you will have your sunshine again."

"Oh pish!" Beth said, as if she had never mentioned how much she missed the sun. "All I want is for you to come back to me safely. That's all I ever want. If you

101

must go, please be careful, Sweetheart. More careful than you have ever been. And please listen to this bright young man. Heed his regard for danger."

Zelie fought off a scowl and nodded.

Sawyer seemed to inflate with pride. "I'll keep her safe," he said.

Beth embraced Sawyer and thanked him over and over. Zelie felt her face pull into a baffled expression but hid it away before Sawyer had a chance to see. Beth kissed her cheek and she smiled. She would play along with this strange charade, for now.

*

In the dim afternoon light, the beanstalk was a dark and gnarled pillar propping up the clouds. The town was mute and still. Curtains were closed and doors locked on all the houses. Swing sets stood motionless, bikes and balls lay abandoned on front lawns. The chimneys puffed weak streams of grey smoke that rose in stripes across the darkened sky.

The loose gravel crunched underfoot, offending the silence, as Sawyer and Zelie approached Mahogany Lane. Now the extent of last night's devastation was clear. The giant's path was marked by uprooted trees, cars squashed pancake flat, light posts bent as if in a forced bow to the self-proclaimed queen and signs crushed, dented or torn into pieces. Most of the terrace houses looked as if they had been through a hurricane. Their jagged remains meekly threatened the dark clouds with wounded defiance. Amongst the shattered wood and bent steel littering the ground, Zelie's backpack lay abandoned upside down and flattened paper-thin against the path. She peeled it up with a sigh and opened the main zip.

Inside the bag, the glue, paint and pieces of gnome had hardened together into a colourful mosaic. Zelie shook her head at the flattened mess and slung it over one shoulder.

The debris grew thicker underfoot as they neared the side of Auntie Ruth's house. The once-ominous fence was a splintered wreck with only a few panels on the far side of the property still standing upright. Zelie stepped her way through what was left of the garden. A movement at the base of the beanstalk caught her eye.

"Dresden!" she shouted, surprised and happy to see the blue gnome had survived. But Dresden did not return her smile. He was hunched over a small pile of shattered red pieces of terracotta.

"Oh no," Sawyer said. "It looks like another one of those gnomes got squashed."

"Was it the giant?" Zelie asked.

Dresden looked up her mutely and then hung his head without even attempting to say a word.

"What's wrong?" asked Sawyer.

"I think it's something to do with the other gnomes," Zelie said. "He can't speak out of turn."

Dresden nodded his head sadly.

"Oh, I might be able to help," said Sawyer. "I had something similar when I was younger but then I had speech therapy."

"Maybe later Sawyer. We had better start climbing. I don't know how long it will take us to get to the top of the beanstalk. Are you ready to go?"

"Wait just one minute," Sawyer said. "I'll go get some supplies."

Zelie murmured her agreement and crouched next to Dresden while Sawyer weaved through the mess of rubble, through the gaping kitchen wall and down through a corridor, out of sight.

"Sawyer and I are going up there," she said to Dresden with an upward glance.

Dresden gave a look of disbelief. He arranged his hands in a point above his head.

"Yes, I know the witch is there and the giant. And Ruth too, but apparently she might actually help us if we can help her first. I think you should come. We need all the help we can get," Zelie said, giving him a significant nod. "And maybe when we get the wand, I can do something about Thurin and Bre."

Dresden flexed his muscles, pointed at the enormous stump and chopped with an invisible axe. He raised his eyebrows, expectantly.

"Jack? —No, he can't come," Zelie said, grimly.

The gnome tapped at his chin in contemplation and then nodded decisively. Together, they collected the broken pieces of Thurin and zipped them into Zelie's backpack alongside the hard flat mess that used to be Bre. Then Dresden leapt on the outside of the backpack like a baby koala.

Sawyer appeared through the broken kitchen and stepped his way around the mounds and craters towards the beanstalk. He had changed into a fresh shirt and a clean jacket. Slung over his shoulder, he carried a backpack of his own. But his expression lacked the certainty she had seen in him earlier. Wringing his hands and glancing intermittently at the sky, he had the look of a lost child.

"What's wrong Sawyer?"

"We're just about to climb the beanstalk. I was just thinking how silly that seems with that giant up there."

"Don't forget the witch with a wand," Zelie added.

Sawyer swallowed thickly and made a high-pitched sound like a leaking tap.

"Maybe you should just stay here," Zelie suggested, in the gentlest voice she could manage.

"Nuh uh," Sawyer said, shaking his head. "I want to

get my Auntie back." He swallowed again. "You don't think Madelene could be expecting us do you?"

"I doubt it. After what the giant did last night, she probably thinks that only a fool would climb up there. But she's wrong."

"So wrong," Sawyer agreed. "It will be three fools."

Dresden bounced with silent laughter.

"You might be right Sawyer," smirked Zelie, finding her first handhold. "I suppose we'd better go find out."

# CHAPTER THIRTEEN

## *Onwards and Upwards*

It had only been half an hour of climbing, but it felt like half a day. Zelie felt certain Sawyer would need to rest before she did, so she pushed herself to keep going. But after only another five minutes, Zelie's muscles were quivering like jelly every time she pulled herself upwards and her grip had become dangerously weak. When exhaustion finally defeated her pride she had no choice but to ask Sawyer for a break. It was a mild consolation to see that he did not even have enough breath for words. In her own struggle, she had not noticed that his jacket was open and his shirt was wet through with sweat. Puffing hard and grimacing, he rolled into the middle of one of the leaves, eyes closed tight with pain.

Dresden was slow to give up his position on Zelie's back. He tested the leaf three times with his foot before he would let go of her. Then he shuffled around on the very centre of the leaf until he seemed satisfied that he was as far from every edge as possible. Even then, he looked thoroughly displeased about being so high above the earth. Having had his feet firmly planted on the ground his whole life, his discomfort was unsurprising. Zelie handed him the back pack with the broken gnomes inside and he crouched and hugged it tightly like a child with a teddy bear.

The leaf under Zelie had a waxy leather surface that conformed to her tired body as if it had been tailored to her precise shape. The wind rocked the leaf ever so gently. On any normal day, it would have made the most luxurious bed feel like a wooden board. Today was no normal day. Everywhere the leaf pressed seemed like torture, reigniting the injuries she had suffered while trying to escape the giant last night. And the effort of climbing had only added to the pain in her muscles and joints. She was used to climbing trees and small hills but nothing like this. Her body felt like it had been run over by a steamroller and now that she had stopped climbing, her scrapes and scratches were stinging with sweat.

Trying to find a position with the least discomfort, Zelie rolled over and took in a view of the village. She could see where Jack's house used to be. There was little left but a crater in the ground surrounded by orange balls which Zelie guessed to be the rest of the pumpkins he had been growing. On the shore, where she had woken up this morning, scattered chunks of debris lay between brown gouges. Small waves were breaking into white foam around the remains of the roof.

Her eyes traced the trampled trails of the giant's destruction leading outwards from the base of the beanstalk across the grey mass of houses. It was almost as if someone had taken an eraser to a pencil sketch of the village and smudged a tangled web of random tracks across it.

Here in the vast space between the still village below and the grey cloud above, a sense of loneliness came over Zelie and she found herself looking over at Sawyer. He still had his eyes closed but his breathing had returned to normal. Despite her suspicion that Sawyer might still wet his pants if somebody said: 'boo!'; how much worse would she feel if she were alone up here? When he opened his eyes, she averted hers and tried to hide the smile that had found its way onto her face. It would be awkward if he got the wrong idea.

She rolled onto her back with a wince and gazed through the enormous leaves. The clouds did not seem to be any closer than when they had begun. If her body did not fall apart sooner, it would take more than a day to climb to the top at this rate. Dresden's weight along with the two other broken gnomes in her back pack had been easy to bear at first. Now it was like carrying a bag of bricks. She dreaded the thought of having that weight on her shoulders again. From here on, their progress would probably be even slower. Even the idea of sitting up was exhausting.

With a forearm draped over her face, Zelie blocked out the world. In her mind, she made a hang glider out of some of the beanstalk leaves and rode off on the winds towards some distant land across the sea. Next, she imagined herself victorious over the witch, parachuting to the ground. Only her parachute was an upside down pair of the giant's trousers with knots tied in the legs. The villagers were cheering. Zelie's mouth pulled into a smile. New thoughts of adventure and magic tumbled into her mind until suddenly, an idea came to her that seemed just plausible enough to try.

"Hey Sawyer, got any rope in that bag?"

Sawyer stirred, having apparently dozed off. He opened one eye, then pressed himself up stiffly and unzipped his pack. After rustling the bag's contents, he pulled out a coil of red rope.

Zelie took it and unwound a short length. "Quite the Boy Scout, aren't you?"

Sawyer shrugged and then put on a dubious look. "What do you need it for?"

"You'll see. If it works, I promise you'll be pleased."

"*If* it works?" Sawyer said. "*If?* This sounds like a harebrained plan to me."

"Ha, harebrained," cried Zelie. "You don't know how close you are."

"Well, I don't want any part of it."

"That's fine. I've got Dresden to help. Don't I Dresden?"

The little blue gnome let go of the back pack and leaped to his feet as if his pants had been electrified. "Can you please run this end of the rope around the beanstalk for me?"

His fear of heights apparently allayed, Dresden snatched the loose end of the rope and pattered off gleefully around the beanstalk.

"Guess everybody likes to feel needed," Sawyer mumbled to himself, while Zelie tied the other end of the rope around her waist.

With a final *patter, patter… thud,* Dresden arrived in front of Zelie, beaming like a dog with a ball.

"Thank you Dresden. You are a super hero," Zelie said, taking the end of the rope and holding it in the crook of her elbow. Dresden bounced on his toes in celebration, while Zelie finished tying her end.

"If you can't tie a knot, tie a lot. Right?" she said.

Sawyer looked at the ugly tangle in Zelie's hands with a mixture of horror and disgust. "What do you call that?"

"It's a bunch of granny knots."

"It looks like a caterpillar swallowed a bag of marbles. Here, let me." His deft fingers disintegrated her knot so swiftly; she never had a chance to object. "Tying a strong knot is easy. Watch." He held the rope firm around her waist and made a loop in one end. "Rabbit goes out of the hole, around the tree and dives back into the hole." As he spoke, he weaved the rope into a neat knot with practiced precision.

"I liked my caterpillar. This rabbit knot looks a bit boring."

"Maybe, but at least this one will hold," Sawyer said, taking the other end and tying it tight around the trunk.

"Well, it's just a precaution anyway. Now, stand back," warned Zelie, kicking the slack rope off the edge of the leaf so it dangled in a long loop below her.

"I hope you've thought this through," Sawyer said, hopping to the next leaf to crouch next to Dresden who was reverse hugging the trunk.

"Thought what through?" Zelie said.

"That's exactly what I mean. How can you be so careless?"

"There's a fine line between careless and clever," she said, trying to sound confident. She could feel her heart pounding on her ribs like a sledgehammer. But her mind was made up. She wiped her sweaty palms on her trousers and gripped the rope so tight, her knuckles cracked.

"Take me up!" Zelie shouted.

With a chime, her hair pulled together into a series of heavy golden cords which slithered upwards into the air like a family of cobras. They hovered for a moment before one of them struck out with a *whoosh,* tightening around the stem of the leaf above her with a light *crumple* sound, like cardboard being folded. Immediately, another cobra whooshed upwards and crumpled around another stem a little higher. Zelie felt her feet lift away the surface of the leaf. The beanstalk foliage parted smoothly. *Whoosh-crumple. Whoosh-crumple.* Zelie whooped with joy, her vision narrowed by an enormous grin as the world flew past her eyes.

Suddenly, the rope around her waist pulled tight

and purred. But her persistent hair continued to pull, stretching her upwards, while the rope cut into her hips, holding her back. She cursed Sawyer's perfect knot through gritted teeth. "Release!" she groaned and her hair immediately fell limp. For a moment she hung in the air, weightless. Then her stomach crawled into her throat as she began to tip backwards.

Head first through the leaves she fell, bashing the leaves with her feet and back. The wind whistled and then screamed in her ears. She clawed at the leaves with numb fingers but they slipped past too quickly to grasp. It was up to Sawyer's knot to save her from plummeting to her death now. It was going to hurt when it pulled tight. She braced her body for the pain. Any moment now. If only she could see, she would be able to tell when. But her hair was blowing around her face, obstructing her vision.

*Her hair!*

"Stop me!" she cried. A tinkling sound rang out above the wind. Her scalp twitched briefly then pulled sharply. Zelie flipped upright and jerked to a violent stop, gasping for air as her legs swung forwards and back.

She found herself only half a body length above the leaf where she had started. Sawyer and Dresden had flattened themselves on one of the leaves and now held identical expressions with wide-eyes and open-mouths. Zelie breathed deeply through an open smile.

"Gosh, that was close," Sawyer said.

"I can't believe it worked!" Zelie exclaimed, admiring the way her hair had spread out in all directions above her, gripping the leaves like a spider's web.

"I don't think you could call that a success," Sawyer said quietly. He was ducking under her feet every time they swung past.

Zelie tugged the knot loose and the rope fell away from her waist, whipping past Sawyer who retrieved it from the trunk indignantly. He wound it up and returned it to his bag.

"That proves it," Zelie said. "Climbing's for suckers. And none of us are suckers, right?"

"Easy to say when you have magic hair."

"You've got magic me," Zelie said with an aerial curtsy. "Do you trust me?"

"With what? —why are you smiling like that—wait, no. I'll climb the normal way."

"Grab them both," Zelie yelled over the end of Sawyer's words. He leaped for safety but it was too late.

Whoosh!

*

For the next 10 minutes, the beanstalk was a green and brown blur. The whooshing and crumpling sounds of Zelie's hair lifting them upwards was rhythmic and strangely soothing.

The hair lasso that had hoisted Sawyer and Dresden off the leaf far below had surprised even Zelie. That same hair had now knitted into something resembling a hammock. And that was where Sawyer and Dresden lay, swaying beneath her feet.

Sawyer shook off his contempt at being, literally, roped into Zelie's crazy plan. "OK," he said. "This is better than climbing. You were right."

Zelie smiled proudly. Now seemed like a good time to ask a question that had been on her mind since Sawyer mentioned it earlier.

"Hey Sawyer, can you remember that spell you got from the witch? That one you said would end the curse on your Auntie."

"Yeah, but it's kinda silly," said Sawyer.

"I don't care. I'd like to hear it. Can you say it for me?"

"If you want. It goes: by the power of this wand and the magic of this bean. Break this curse's bond and let nature supervene."

"Supervene?" Zelie said.

"It's when something unexpected comes along and makes things change in an important way," Sawyer said. "I didn't know the word either. I had to look it up."

"So you need a bean and a wand and the spell to break the curse?" Zelie said. "Any curse at all?"

Dresden began nodding as if he knew the answer.

"I think so. I never got a chance to try it," said Sawyer.

They were dizzyingly high above the village now. The distant crushed tracks of destruction carved out by the giant looked as tiny and intricate as an electrical circuit amongst the jumble of small rectangular houses.

As they ascended, Sawyer became silent and stared blankly while he twisted the leg of his pants. Somehow, Zelie knew how he was feeling. A niggling fear was twisting inside her belly too, like a tightening screw. Above the cloud was a mystery. As far as they knew, only the giant and the witch had ever seen it and returned to the village alive. Even Dresden seemed to feel the tension and began chewing at his knuckles.

Though the leaves of the beanstalk hindered her view, she could tell that the ceiling of her world was closer than it had ever been. They were only a few minutes from breaking through the cloud. But their progress had been slowing gradually and the *whoosh-crumple* of her hair had begun to sound as tired as Zelie felt herself. It was as if her energy was being sapped by the magic driving her hair. Her eyelids were drooping heavily when Sawyer roused her.

113

"Um, Zelie.

"Mmm?"

"How will we rescue Auntie? I mean, how do we get her away from Madelene?" Sawyer's voice was quiet as if he thought he might be heard above the cloud.

Zelie groaned. "I don't know yet. Let's just wait and see."

A thick silence fell between them. But Zelie was too exhausted to care. Then Sawyer made a series of soft high squeaks, rousing her once again. Scowling down at Sawyer, she saw the muscles in his neck drawn tight with the effort of suppressing a full cry. For some reason this was infuriating.

"Look Sawyer, you had your chance to stay behind and you didn't take it. You're here now, so don't go turning into a pile of pudding right when you have a chance to be useful."

Sawyer's face darkened. "Pudding?" he snarled, surprising Zelie with his ferocity. "How many giants and witches have you taken on before? They could be waiting for us with five other giants and zombie slaves or mutant rats. And if she can add an extra thumb to my hand, she can probably tear off our arms just by blinking." And on he went, his scathing tone soon withering into a wavering whine.

Zelie's first instinct was to retort, but she could not pry her tense jaw open to speak. On the surface she was burning with rage. But deep down she was also more frightened than she had ever been. Her heart began to drum in her chest. She breathed in and out loudly through her nose.

Sawyer had moved on to describe a huge spider with poisonous boils all over its body that the witch might have turned herself into. She cut him off sharply.

"Stop, Sawyer. Just stop. You're not making it any

easier."

Sawyer fell silent, but he had already picked a scab in Zelie's mind that she had been determined to leave alone. And now it began to ooze nightmarish thoughts and fearful questions. Images flashed in her mind so vividly that they might have been memories. A line of small children chained together, scrubbing the wooden floor of an enormous ballroom. Beth running along the street in the looming shadow of the giant's enormous foot. Then Auntie Ruth pleading for her life at the feet of a dark figure that Zelie took to be the witch.

The thought of Ruth in danger troubled Zelie more than she expected it might. Naturally, she wanted her mother to be free of harm and she hated the thought of children as slaves. But why did she care at all for Auntie Ruth? Despite what Jack had said, the dried up old hag seemed at least as evil and selfish as the witch, just less powerful. And of course, they had at least one house-crushing giant. And who did Zelie have on her side? A terracotta man and a timid boy. Not exactly an even fight, was it? This adventure could be over in a matter of moments if the giant was up there waiting to swat them from the beanstalk. Would he brag to the witch about squashing all of them in one go?

The enormity of this challenge began to dawn on Zelie. What if the witch was as supremely skilled with magic as she would have everybody believe? She could cast a spell with the wave of her hand and turn them all into insects. Ruth would love that. She would squash them under her boot without even needing an order. A feeling of despair entered Zelie and she began to hope for mercy. If there was any kindness in the witch's heart, perhaps she would turn Zelie into something unique like a ladybird before she became goo on the sole of Ruth's shoe.

No. Zelie pushed those thoughts away with a hard blink. If she kept this up she could end up a shaky mess like Sawyer. She had to think like Jack. What would he say at a time like this?

Jack. And that's when she pictured him, unconscious in the ambulance, blood seeping through his bandages, thrashing under the influence of that concoction, and all because of her clumsiness and curiosity.

She had to fix this. If she failed, the witch would have no impediment and could inflict on her friends and family whatever terrible torture her black heart desired. It was not really a choice. Something had to be done. And she could not do it on her own.

OK, she thought, Sawyer needs to hear a plan. What can I tell him? What have we got on our side? "We'll stay hidden," Zelie said to Sawyer, finally. "They don't know we're coming so we can't let them see us. We'll find out where they keep that wand. And as soon as we have it, we can save your Auntie."

"Then can we go home?" Sawyer asked.

"After your Auntie ends the curse. And puts the witch in chains. Oh, and changes the giant back so Jack can have a brother again."

"Oh," said Sawyer. "All of that?"

"Yes, I suppose it's a lot. But we can't do any of it unless you stop thinking up all the ways it could go wrong and start helping me. Do you think you can do that?"

Sawyer looked up from where he had been toying with Zelie's hair hammock. "Alright," he said with a tinge of doubt in his voice.

The air was growing cold and moist as they rose towards the dark cloud. Its lower surface stretched off into the distance like an upside down wasteland. Zelie

116

could see an opening in the cloud above them now. But it was not gleaming with the blinding light she had expected. It was pitch black and brought her a cold sense of doom. As they rose smoothly inside, her eyes dropped to Sawyer who looked almost as tiny and scared as Dresden in the darkening shadow. The light slipped away and left them blind, damp and cold. But Zelie could feel that they were still rising and with every inch her fists balled tighter and tighter.

# CHAPTER FOURTEEN

## *Through the Cloud*

Once they were inside the hole, it was so dark that Zelie could not tell if her eyes were open or shut. Moisture formed droplets on her cheeks that trickled down her neck and along her arms before escaping from her fingertips and falling off into the darkness. As her clothes became wet, the fabric closed in with sticky cold fingers. The whoosh-crumple of her hair grabbing at the leaves was the only sound apart from Sawyer's breathing which had become noticeably quicker.

"I'm scared too," Zelie admitted into the darkness. She felt Sawyer squeeze her foot and she was embarrassed to be trembling. Dresden tightened his hold on her back.

The air began to feel warmer, almost steamy, and smelled of fresh rain. Grey light eased through the darkness, steadily revealing the shadowy contours of passing leaves.

"Slow down. Keep quiet. Stay hidden," she called softly to her hair. The crisp whoosh-crumple of her hair diminished to a lazy squelch, like a soapy sponge being squeezed of its bubbles, each time it tightened around a stem.

Spears of light began to twinkle through the shadows. The edges of the leaves glowed green. Hints of the most brilliant blue flashed through the waving foliage and Zelie's jaw fell open.

The sky was more vivid with colour than she had

ever imagined possible. Her heart felt like a velvet wave. The rim of the cloud was so bright and white it made her eyes water. She dipped her head to avert her teary gaze and caught a glimpse of Sawyer, staring up in awe. Though his clothes and hair were soaked to his skin, they shone bright and full with colours that had been invisible below the cloud. His cheeks showed a hint of pink, while flecks of orange shone in his brown eyes. Dresden rested his chin over her shoulder and hummed.

Up through the hole with squinting eyes Zelie spied the tips of two dark thin spires, like poison needles pressed hard against the blue sky. Each spire descended to a triangular roof over a circular tower of shoddily placed stone. The towers held oddly shaped windows which gazed out of the castle like a pair of sad eyes. A balcony connected the towers, but it sat on an angle as if it had sunk on one side. Below the balcony was a huge timber panel which looked to be made of household doors hammered roughly together. Leading up to the castle was a wide row of stone steps and an open platform, like a large stage.

As her body emerged from the cloud, the unfamiliar brightness forced Zelie's eyes into narrow slits. The sudden dry heat on her face was like an open oven. Sawyer gasped as he rose up beneath her. And finally, there it was: the sun—a blissful orange ball of light and warmth hovering majestically beside the castle, like a holy orb.

A movement beneath the sun distracted her eye. A dark mound on the cloud surface to the left of the castle. It rose and fell, up and down. Huge feet jutted from one end. Hairy shoulders peeked from the other.

*The giant.*

A balloon of air—a scream—erupted inside Zelie.

She trapped it with a tiny squawk. As if sensing her distress, her hair jerked sideways violently and hauled her around the trunk of the beanstalk out of view. Sawyer swung wildly beneath her, rustling the leaves as he brushed past.

Zelie's body was numb and wet but her cheeks were hot as she stared blankly across the seemingly endless white cloud on the hidden side of the beanstalk. Undeterred, her hair continued as instructed, squelching slowly upwards towards a deep blue inverted ocean.

"Stop," she squeaked through her tightened throat. Her hair froze in place. One of the snake-like tendrils even paused mid-strike. It happened so suddenly that she bounced up and down a few times before coming to a standstill.

"That wasn't the giant, was it?" Sawyer whispered. He sounded more curious now than frightened. And without waiting for an answer, he hopped onto the nearest leaf. It was roughly half the size of the leaves below the cloud but it held Sawyer's weight just fine. "Oh my gosh, yes. That's him," Sawyer confirmed, peering around the beanstalk. He sounded buoyant. "But he looks so much smaller, doesn't he? Look at that. I never thought of him having to sleep. Did you?"

But Zelie could not think. She was suddenly so incredibly tired that it was barely possible to re-open her eyes each time she blinked. She reached out to a nearby leaf and spun herself towards the trunk.

"You look sick?" said Sawyer, his voice a breathy whisper. "Are you going to be alright?"

"It's just my hair," she mumbled flatly. "I think it uses up my energy."

"Oh, OK. Well, what should we do?"

"I gotta get down from here. Off you get little man,"

Zelie said.

Sawyer reached up to help Dresden down off her back while Zelie looked for something to hold on to. The trunk of the beanstalk was green and smooth above the cloud, as if this part of the plant was still young and had not yet hardened. Zelie could see where the two stems met. She put her fingers into the groove. But as her hair released and fluttered behind her, her grip gave way. If not for Sawyer guiding her inwards, she would have fallen back through the hole in the cloud. She flopped onto the leaf like a sheet of heavy rubber.

For a few minutes, she lay on her side until the bright white cloud dimmed to a deep orange, creased with shadows. The sun was setting but it was on the castle-side of the beanstalk. After all Jack's talk of sunsets, she had to see one with her own eyes. Summoning all of her strength, she rolled her depleted body over and dragged herself across the leaves with all the speed of a snail through peanut butter.

The sun had just kissed the cloud's horizon right over where the giant lay snoring between the castle and what looked to be a barn. She stared unblinking as the sun eased inside the horizon, fading to a deep red, and shrinking to a gleaming slither. When it finally disappeared, the heat on Zelie's face seeped away and new colours blossomed in the sky. Orange and red and blue and purple and pink, intertwined like a harmony of light. Between slow blinks, Zelie watched the colours gradually fade.

She melted into the leaf's smooth surface, keeping only one eye open. In the haze that precedes sleep, her blurred gaze drifted to the giant, with his feet poking towards the beanstalk under a blanket that looked like an ancient sail from a yacht. The beige mound rose and fell steadily in time with his loud snores. A vague

121

thought passed through Zelie's brain as she closed her eyes. Sawyer was right. He did seem smaller. A lot smaller. Although perhaps the twilight and distance were playing tricks on her tired mind.

*

Zelie awoke with a jolt. Auntie Ruth's voice was like broken glass inside her head.

"Wake up you lazy brute. The queen wants you by the window," she screeched at the giant.

Sawyer and Dresden shuffled in behind Zelie as her eyes came into focus on Auntie Ruth holding up a burning torch to light her way in the twilight. The giant was taller lying on his side than Ruth was standing up. But Zelie was certain now that he was so much smaller than he had looked under the street lights. How could he possibly have the strength to throw Jack's house?

Ruth swung back her leg and kicked the giant with a nasty thud. The giant snuffled and snorted briefly and returned to his rhythmic snoring.

Muttering, Ruth walked away, hung the torch on the castle wall, and picked up a broom that was leaning nearby. "I said, wake up!" she screamed as she ran with the broom like a pole vaulter, jamming the end into the giant's ribs with an echoing thump. Zelie grimaced. She pulled up the edge of the leaf and peered over the top.

The giant pushed up on one arm and thundered: "Fee—Fi-"

"Fo, fum. Yes, yes, I know," Ruth said, impatiently. "Just get over there. Go on." She pointed at the castle.

The giant laboured to his feet and lumbered in the direction of the pointed finger, turning to face Zelie.

"See, he looks so much smaller, doesn't he?" whispered Sawyer over her shoulder.

"Yes," Zelie agreed. "Hey, look at you. Not a hint of pudding in sight."

Sawyer seemed to accept this as a compliment and adopted a proud expression.

There were three windows in the round corner tower of the castle: low, middle and high. The giant plodded over and turned his ear to the middle window, showing the obedience of a trained dog. With his jaw slack, tongue lolling to the edge of his rubbery lips and eyes rolled half-way inside his eyelids, his swollen face looked vacant of any thought.

"He's ready, your highness," Auntie Ruth squawked.

Then the chanting began. The voice was hypnotic and strangely soothing, echoing out of the castle as if it was being announced in a church with high ceilings.

*"This little boy is weak and tiny:*
*Skin and bones, his voice is whiney.*
*This little boy is like a twig.*
*This little boy ought to be big.*
*So make him huge and very strong.*
*Make him ugly; make him pong.*
*No longer scrawny, make him brawny,*
*Enormous, scary, tall and hairy,*
*Large and tough and slow and dumb.*
*Make him boom Fee-Fi-Fo-Fum."*

As the spell cascaded from the window, the giant's body swelled and rose up, up, up, past the top window and towards the roof. His face puffed up until it was all nose and lips and forehead and his eyes were just dark holes in his face. Hairs sprouted on his shoulders and chest, like the claws of a cat. By the time the spell finished, the castle looked like a doll's house next to him.

The giant tilted his face to the sky and released an unholy gargling howl that Zelie felt vibrating in her chest. The giant's cry was lingering and filled with a strange sorrow, like a tortured animal.

"Oh no," whispered Zelie.

# CHAPTER FIFTEEN

## *The Witch Appears*

The spell had rounded the giant's shoulders, bringing them level with his ears. But even hunched over, he stood taller than the castle roof. Auntie Ruth stood just barely the height of the giant's ankle now. She cowered against the castle tower, trying to avoid the huge globs of sticky drool that were stretching from the giant's loose lips and splotching on the cloud. A circle of ice crystals spread out on the wall from where Ruth pressed her back.

Any courage within Sawyer had evaporated now. His soft whine itched in Zelie's ear like a mosquito's buzz. Zelie gave a nudge to quiet him and received an elbow in return, awaking a bruise on her ribs she did not know she had.

The giant twitched his nose, seeming to smell something. Then with a deep gargle, he took a heavy stride towards the wooden barn. Zelie braced for the rumble of impact but the giant's foot landed in silence. Waves rippled outwards from the giant's foot along the cloud surface, tripping Auntie Ruth onto her hands.

The giant dropped to one knee, sending out more silent ripples, and levered the barn doors open with a huge fingernail. His titanic hand slid inside the opening, splintering off one of the doors as if it were made of balsa wood. He rummaged briefly inside and then withdrew his hand. Pinched between thumb and forefinger he held a fully grown sheep, bleating hysterically.

"No no no!" cried an exasperated Auntie Ruth. She found her feet, grabbed the broom she had used to wake the giant, and threw it. The broom skimmed the giant's leg and scuttled across the cloud's surface.

Oblivious to Ruth's screeching and broom-throwing, the giant tossed the sheep in the air and caught it deep in his throat, swallowing it whole like a grape. Auntie Ruth grabbed another tool off the wall of the castle, which Zelie only recognised as a garden fork after Ruth had buried its prongs into the side of the giant's big toe.

"Huh?" the giant grunted, as if Ruth had simply tapped him on the shoulder.

"No more! You eat down in the village, you foul ogre! Not here," Auntie Ruth screeched. She shot a desperate glance back at the castle. But apparently the damage was done.

A spear of electricity shot from the castle window with a loud crackle and hit Auntie Ruth in the centre of her back. At the same time, another crooked beam of light cut a hole through the back wall of the castle and forked into the sky, sending castle bricks tumbling to the cloud surface. Auntie Ruth arched her back in pain and slumped forwards against the giant's foot. Smoke enveloped her as the thunder boomed and the beanstalk shuddered.

Sawyer retreated and, for a moment, Zelie thought he might have gone off to hide his head between his knees. But he quickly reappeared on the leaf below hers with Dresden at his side. They were simply after a better view.

The heavy wooden door of the castle clicked and then slid sideways with a mechanical whirr. A small smirking woman with a very upright posture, glided out so smoothly she might have been on wheels. She wore a battered gold crown over carefully groomed hair, an emerald gown with deep red and gold trim which glimmered as she moved. This had to be the witch.

Auntie Ruth wrestled her body off the cloud and onto her haunches facing away from the stranger and rubbed at a blackened area on her back where the lightning had struck.

"I tried to tell him, Highness. I said he shouldn't. But he wouldn't stop," Ruth said. Her screeching voice had a fearful waver to it. "You know how he is. Doesn't listen, does he?"

"I do not care for excuses. It is your job to prevent pilferage. Is that so difficult to understand," the witch said, smoothly.

"Your grace," grunted Ruth, still in obvious pain. "I'm sure I'd do better if only… well, if I knew what that word meant. Please, my queen, what is 'pilf-ah-ridge'?"

"It means that the monster has obtained what was not his to take. This is the second time since I put him in your charge. Is it a necessity that I tell you everything twice?"

"Yes ma'am, I mean no ma'am. I'll do better. Please forgive me Madelene. I-"

"Insolence!"

"*Queen* Madelene. That's what I meant," Ruth said in a rush, looking fearfully over one shoulder with an elbow guarding her face. "Beg your merciful pardon, most gracious highness," Ruth grovelled.

The witch opened her great coat to reveal several brightly-coloured vials affixed to a woven leather belt around her waist. Ruth's eyes widened in fear. The witch took out a blue vial, uncorked it and then seemed to change her mind and slotted it back into her belt with an exasperated sigh.

"I shan't waste good potions on the likes of you."

"Oh, thank you, merciful majesty," Ruth fawned.

"But if you *ever* disrespect me like that again, I'll turn your tongue into a cactus," said the witch with a scowl, turning to face the castle as she fastened her coat closed. "You must exercise control."

"Yes, Highness."

"Both over the language you use to address me and over our perpetually recalcitrant companion," she said, with a gesture towards the giant that looked more like a shudder than a wave.

"Of course. Yes. Yes, I will remember that my queen."

"You will, indeed," Madelene said, and, with the faintest hint of a smile, turned and held the wand up like a javelin pointed at Ruth. "And I shall help you."

"Oh, thank you your ladyship," Ruth said, relieved. But when she saw the wand her voice rose to a piercing shriek. "No, please not like that. I'll remember. I will-"

"Offences against the crown must not go unpunished. Do *NOT...* let it *HAPPEN... AGAIN!*" Three successive lightning bolts shot out of the wand and struck Ruth in the rump making her stiffen and fall forwards. Matching streaks of lightning shot from other end of the wand cutting jagged diagonal scars across the face of the castle up into the dark sky.

Ruth's convulsing body drove out a quavering howl as the electricity escaped through her. The cloud beneath her flickered. Thunder crackled and rolled away until it disappeared and only the sound of Auntie Ruth's weak moaning could be heard as she lay deflated and still.

The giant seemed unaware of the quarrel at his feet. This whole time, he had been merrily plucking animals from the barn one at a time, flicking them skywards as they bleated, mooed and oinked, and gulping them down noisily.

"As for you, Monster," Madelene said with a spooky calmness. "How many times must I remind you? Those animals are property of the throne." She directed the wand at the colossal frame of the giant. With a gasp, Zelie saw that the other end of the wand was pointed right at her and she rolled behind the trunk of the beanstalk, burying her head as several bolts of electricity fizzed and sizzled past.

Just inches above Zelie's head, a smoking hole hissed and popped. It smelled of boiled cabbage. One of the lightning bolts had drilled right through the beanstalk trunk leaving a hole big enough to fit a tennis ball. White, boiling sap bubbled and danced out of the hole. It dribbled down the trunk towards Sawyer and Dresden who were curled up together in a ball. The lightning had sliced off the outer half of their leaf but seemed to have missed all flesh, bone, paint and clay. Sawyer gave her an astonished grin as the booming thunder diminished into a distant echo.

Glancing back towards the barn, Zelie saw Madelene, hands on hips, surveying her handiwork. Wisps of smoke rose from the giant who had collapsed onto his side and was rolling side to side clutching his blackened backside. The breeze brought Zelie the smell of burned hair. It took her a moment to find Ruth who was almost entirely embedded in the cloud beside the giant.

"And thus, order is restored," Madelene said, with an air of satisfaction in her voice, as she slotted the wand into the pocket of her coat.

The scene before Zelie, gave her a sudden moment of clarity. The witch was little more than a well-dressed bully. No wonder the wand only shot out lightning for her. She could not conjure a kind gesture for all the castles and servants in the world.

A rustle of leaves beneath Zelie, drew her attention. To her astonishment, a man's head popped up through the hole. He surveyed the landscape carefully and then, with a sudden jerk, disappeared back into the blackness of the hole.

"Monster!" Madelene cried and Zelie realised at once that the man had been seen. The giant propped himself up on his elbows with groggy obedience. "Up," ordered Madelene and the giant obeyed, barely missing Auntie Ruth's unconscious body as he fought for balance. For a moment of silence, Madelene stared towards the beanstalk with a palm raised at the giant. The giant twisted some fluff from inside his belly button and then ate it.

Then out of the corner of her eye, Zelie spotted the man's head emerge from the shadows and steal another glance at Madelene.

"Seize that man," Madelene said, pointing.

Zelie's eyes widened, her heart drummed and she edged out of view.

The stranger disappeared down into the darkness of the hole once more. Zelie hoped he could climb better than he could hide. The giant's strides were clumsy but quick. He fell to his knees beside the beanstalk causing a large wave to radiate outwards in all directions. The wave shook the castle on its way towards Madelene and Ruth. When it reached Madelene, she shot straight up in the air—expressionless and with her hands still on her hips—as if a hidden wire were elevating her. Up and back down in a straight line she went, returning to the surface of the cloud like a stick into mud. Auntie Ruth did exactly the opposite. Her limp body flipped, flopped and bounced to a twisted unconscious sprawl.

The giant plunged his long arm into the dark hole so deep that his shoulder nudged the beanstalk, rocking Zelie from her perch and sending her crashing down onto Sawyer and Dresden's leaf. Her nose was inches from the red hot edge where the lightning had cleft it. Sawyer clasped her arm and pulled her to safety.

The man's muffled yell sounded from deep inside the hole and the giant withdrew his wet arm, revealing the man's tiny head, squeezed purple. Inside the giant's white-knuckled fist, veins bulged on the man's grimacing face.

Zelie drew a sharp breath. "Jack!" she said in a breathy whisper. How was it even possible?

The giant gave another squeeze, expelling a grunt from Jack. Zelie had never seen such pain on his face. Anger and helplessness boiled inside her. Sawyer clapped a hand across her mouth just in time to catch her scream.

"Max no. It's me," Jack strained inside the giant's tight grip. "It's Jack." The giant became still. His eyes were glazed and lifeless. But Zelie was sure she saw colour return to the giant's knuckles. Had he consciously loosened his grip or had he simply run out of commands from the witch?

"Let me see him, Monster," Madelene commanded.

The giant pivoted to face Madelene, but not before he had disgorged a moist grunt in Zelie's direction. She grasped the edge of the leaf tightly as the gust made it bluster about. Like a cowboy on an angry bull, she held on for dear life. The choking stench of rotten, warm giant's breath filled her nostrils and stung her eyes.

"I know this man," said Madelene cocking her head, amused. "Spriggins isn't it? The one who cut down my beanstalk and helped Ruth cast me into the sea?"

"Please Max," Jack groaned, ignoring Madelene. The

131

giant was still except for a thin stream of drool which leaked from the side of his mouth and stretched towards the cloud. Madelene sniggered through her upturned nose.

"Did you call him 'Max'? Oh, you are much mistaken. He has no name. He is simply, Monster," she said proudly. She pulled the wand from her pocket and strode past Jack with it clasped in both hands behind her back. "But this is no random name: Max. You seem to know him. How would that be?"

"He's my brother?" Jack struggled out.

"Your brother?" Madelene exclaimed with glee. "Oh glorious retribution. Well, Spriggins. I'd say it was a fairly even swap: my beanstalk for your sibling."

"Why doesn't he remember me?" Jack grunted.

"Complex thoughts and past memories would have impeded his duty, so I repressed them," Madelene explained, loftily. "Without those extraneous faculties, he is my royal and loyal subject, the brawn to my brains, ready to efficiently and unquestioningly enact my will. He has no mind except to obey me. I alone command him."

Jack squirmed. "A brainless slave? But why would you-"

"Because I am queen," she snapped, as if the question offended her. For a moment she seemed upset with herself for having lost her temper. As if to ease her tension, she stretched her neck in a way that looked as if she were drawing a large circle with her nose. "Blind obedience is a servant's function. If my subjects did not obey, what sort of queen would that make me? Hmm?" She paced around the giant as she talked. "In hindsight, perhaps my spell should have required him to retain saliva in his mouth rather than spilling it all over my cloud. However, tomorrow, I shall have a fresh cohort of servants. And then I can do away with this monster and that freezing, squawking excuse for a royal butler," she sneered, fluttering her hand in Ruth's direction. "In the meantime, reminding them who's boss is infinitely simpler now that I have this little treasure." She twirled the wand and smiled.

Jack wore a scowl.

"I see the remorse in your eyes, Spriggins," Madelene said. "A traitor's sadness can be a heavy burden. But don't worry. You won't have to carry it any longer. I shall help you." She paused underneath Jack and bounced on her toes. Zelie had a bad feeling. Apparently, so did Jack because his writhing became frantic inside the giant's grasp.

"Let me be," he laboured.

Madelene put up her palm to him. "The people know you as the man who defied a queen, Spriggins. They commend your bravery and your rebellion and that will not do."

"Max!" Jack pleaded.

"You shall be made an example. Resistance shall not be tolerated," Madelene continued. "Monster, you may kill him now," she ordered with a wave of her hand. Her voice rose at the end, as if she had wasted too much time, as if Jack were just an inconvenience, an interruption to her schedule. The giant let out a huff, blowing Jack's hair back. Jack wrinkled his face and coughed sharply.

With a violent swing of his outstretched arm, the giant whipped Jack at the surface of the cloud, spraying an arc of water into the air as Jack's wet clothes gave up the moisture they had absorbed on his ascent up the beanstalk. He rebounded off the clouds surface as if it were a trampoline. High into the air he flew, bouncing again and again until he stopped, stunned but somehow uninjured.

"Down the hole, Monster," Madelene instructed impatiently, gesturing to where the beanstalk protruded through the cloud. "Throw—him—down—the—hole."

Jack found his feet quickly, ducked the giant's wild swipe and then, bounding awkwardly across the cloud, he launched himself at Madelene. With a casual step sideways, Madelene dodged his tackle, sighed at the giant, then swivelled and raised the wand at Jack.

Lightning flashed from the wand and fizzed by Jack as he rolled out of the way. At the same time a jagged electrical spear sprang from the other end of the wand, frying a sooty crater in the giant's lower leg.

The giant let out a deep gurgled scream and gripped his leg in pain and then hopped around, sending large waves rippling across the cloud with every landing. Madelene took aim at Jack again but before she could fire another shot, one of the waves ran at her from behind and launched her skywards. Jack followed her up into the air.

Madelene rose and fell smoothly, just as she had before. Only this time, she fired the wand over and over at Jack's somersaulting body and by some miracle, missed every time. Her face looked calm, almost bored, until she landed directly on the face of an oncoming wave.

With a shriek, she flipped upside down. Her legs shot straight up in the air and her gown fell over her head. Madelene's pale legs flailed wildly as the self-proclaimed queen fought to restore her dignity. She had just gripped the hem of her gown and pulled it below her chin when she landed directly on her head and rebounded, tumbling into a wild twisting spin that would have inspired jealousy from an Olympic diving champion.

Meanwhile, the giant continued to hop and gargle in pain and Ruth's unconscious body was drawn into the trampoline show. In the chaos, the wand and Madelene's battered crown were catapulted way up into the air. The crown descended around one of the castle spires like a quoit, while the wand deflected off the roof and fell between Madelene and Jack.

Jack continued to bounce, though he never took his eyes off the wand. Zelie's heart raced and, inexplicably, tears sprang to her eyes. He might win his freedom, if only he could grab the wand and turn it on Madelene. Zelie's fingers ached from gripping the leaf so tightly. "Get it, Jack. Get it," she whispered. A number of times, the wand came maddeningly close to Jack's outstretched fingers but, on the next bounce, drew farther away.

"Seize him, Monster," came Madelene's muffled cry from beneath her regal frock.

The giant, still holding onto his leg, hopped after Jack but tripped on one of the waves that had rebounded off the castle. He fell onto his side creating the largest wave yet. It whipped along the cloud surface and flicked all three trampolinists way up in the sky. As Madelene tumbled head over shiny black heels, her dress rode up even further, revealing a pair of pink underwear. Zelie giggled softly and sniffed.

The giant got to his knees. The wand drifted closer to Jack. And then, when he was upside down in mid-somersault, he lashed out a hand and grabbed the wand. But the very next instant, the giant snatched him out of the sky and hurled him through the hole in the cloud. Jack's muffled yell faded quickly into silence.

Zelie's breath caught in her throat. Jack was falling, leaves bashing against his back, the way they had on hers earlier in the day. But he had neither rope nor magic hair to save him. Her jaw trembled and tears flooded her eyes. Seeing Jack somehow cured of his injuries, she had allowed herself a moment of desperate hope. But now that had been torn away.

Zelie blinked away the tears and glared with gritted teeth. The giant stood awaiting instructions as the waves diminished to a gentle roll across the cloud. Madelene came to a stop and unhitched her gown. Seeing her delicately patting her hair into place caused something inside Zelie to snap.

Hot fury erupted like volcano inside her. With fists balled tight, she pushed herself up. But then Sawyer's weight was on top of her and his hand over her mouth.

"No," he said in a distressed whisper as she struggled to get free. "No. You said we would stay hidden. Stop struggling, will you. Come on. You saw what happened to Jack. Please—please, don't leave me here like this."

She squeezed her eyes shut and pushed her forehead into the leaf. Sawyer puffed out his captive breath and released his grip slowly.

"It's not fair," she murmured, her voice low and gravelly. Hot tears dripped from her eyes onto the leaf, then rolled and fell silently off the edge, following Jack down the dark and dreadful hole.

# CHAPTER SIXTEEN

## *Hidden in the Shadows*

Having received no further instructions from Madelene, the giant stood motionless, staring blankly at the hole at the base of the beanstalk through which he had flung the screaming Jack. Madelene seemed dizzy after all those bouncing somersaults and it took her a while to regain enough composure to stand. Satisfied that Jack had been dispatched, she ordered the giant behind the castle. "Sit there until you are summoned," she commanded. The brute obeyed while Madelene bounced up and down on his waves, smoothing down her gown and pinching at her eyelashes as if to make them perfectly parallel. She shot a glance at her crown, impaled on one of the castle spires, and then at the giant. Then apparently abandoning the idea of asking him to retrieve her royal hat, she glided over to where Ruth still lay sprawled on the cloud.

After rousing Ruth with a cruel kick, Madelene shouted orders about planting fruit trees and vegetables for the children and then waddled into the castle with her nose held aloft. Ruth hobbled after Madelene and pulled a lever inside the castle causing the timber door to whirr and rumble across the opening until it arrived in its final position with a loud clunk.

As Zelie glared at the giant, dribbling on his knees with his back against the castle, she wondered if his mind was capable of generating a single thought for himself. It struck her that he was able to produce little other than drool without an instruction.

Rather than despair, a numbness came over Zelie as she realised the wand was gone. Jack had been holding it when he was thrown down the hole. Without it, Zelie could not reverse the spell on Ruth. And Ruth was the only one who was sure to have the skill necessary to lift the curse.

Zelie's face was hot and tight from dry tears. Too tired to cry any more, she closed her eyes while Dresden rubbed a soothing hand on her back.

\*

Zelie had fallen asleep. When she awoke, the gluey feeling in her mouth and the dryness of her clothes told her it had been hours. Rolling onto her back, she rubbed her bleary eyes open. She had a vague sense of a bluish black curtain adorned with millions of twinkling pinpricks but as her eyes lost their sleepy haze, she found herself scanning the sky from horizon to horizon, in awe of the array of sparkling lights that decorated it. She had little time to appreciate this new wonder because from somewhere very close, a deep, resonant voice scared her tense.

"Cloud," it boomed. A quick glance toward the castle showed the giant still dribbling in his place beside the castle. She released a sigh of relief. Then she saw Dresden and Sawyer sitting on the leaf adjacent hers. Sawyer appeared to be whispering in the gnome's ear.

"S- sun," stuttered Dresden.

"Hello," she whispered.

"Oh good, you're awake" Sawyer said, spinning to face her. "Feeling better?"

"A little." She gestured to the sky. "What do you make of that?"

"You mean the stars," Sawyer said.

"Stars," parroted Dresden, proudly.

"Is that what they're called?" said Zelie. "With all the fuss about the sun, nobody ever told me about stars."

"I read about them," Sawyer said quietly. "There's even a song called 'Twinkle Twinkle Little Star' but I can't remember how it goes."

"Twinkle," said Dresden.

"Some people believe you turn into a star when you die," continued Sawyer. "I think those two over there might be my Mum and Dad."

As Zelie gazed at the sky, a particularly bright star caught her eye and the thought of Jack renewed itself in her mind. The sadness wormed its way back into Zelie's heart and the night sky became blurry as fresh tears welled in her eyes.

Sawyer shuffled over and squeezed her with one arm. "Well, maybe you'll like the moon, instead." Sawyer suggested. "It's supposed to look like an enormous glowing orb."

"Mmmmooo," Dresden attempted.

"Gosh, little man, you've got to keep it down." Sawyer warned. He leaned around the beanstalk and gave a relieved sigh. "That giant must be a heavy sleeper."

Zelie gave the gnome a nod. "It's good to hear your voice again, Dresden."

The gnome gave her a grin.

"I've been doing speech therapy stuff with him," Sawyer said. "He seems to want to tell us something. I think he knows more than we do. After all, the gnomes have been in the garden long before the curse, maybe they know the witch's weaknesses."

At this, Dresden began flailing his arms about as if he was shaping things in the air and moving them about. It was a kind of sign language.

"He did this before," said Sawyer. "I just don't know what you mean, Dresden."

Dresden waved his arms around in an even more frantic fashion and pointed up in the air and at the castle and then down towards the ground.

Sawyer and Zelie exchanged confused glances. Puffing out a sigh, Dresden put his palms to the sky as if he had tried all he could.

Zelie's stomach rumbled loudly. Sawyer's shoulders shot up to his ears and he checked the giant again.

"Sorry about that," whispered Zelie, pressing both hands into her stomach.

"You're hungry," Sawyer observed. He fumbled in his bag and withdrew a handful of food. With a primal grunt, she snatched it right out of his hands and stuffed it into her mouth. Though it was only a few strips of salty dried beef, to Zelie nothing had tasted sweeter. Sawyer held out an open bottle. "Drink?"

The water could not flow fast enough and Zelie's gulps were loud and large.

"Sounds like a seal choking on a fish bone, eh little man?" Sawyer said, nudging his little blue companion.

Dresden snorted a laugh through his nose and Zelie gave Sawyer a beefy smirk. He was actually quite funny. Zelie was both surprised and strangely relieved. She took a bite out of an apple and then shook her head, putting the apple aside and quickly filling her mouth with more tasty beef.

"Is there any more of this?" she said, almost spilling her mouthful.

"That's the last of the salted stuff," Sawyer said, looking a little worried. "Maybe you'll find some fresh beef in that barn. You know, the kind that goes *moo*."

Zelie chuckled and inhaled a piece of the beef,

which sent her into a coughing fit.

Sawyer thumped on her back and apologised and pleaded with her to keep quiet. She did her best to muffle the sound in the sleeve of her jacket. But it did no good.

The giant snorted awake. "Fee—Fi—Fo—Fum," he bellowed.

Zelie finally dislodged the piece of beef and scrambled out of the giant's line of sight.

"I smell the blood of an Englishman!" the giant bellowed a few moments later. His voice was already close and he sounded as if he was moving around towards them. With the cloud under his feet, his footsteps were silent. Unless he sniffed, grunted or spoke, there was no telling where he was. Luckily, the giant seemed to be in a talkative mood.

"Be he alive, or be he dead," roared the giant.

Zelie and the others scurried to keep the beanstalk between them and the giant.

"Or be—he—dead," the giant repeated, then faltered, muttering, "er—um,"

By now Zelie was aware that she and the others were in full view of the castle so, naturally, they jumped with fright when, from the balcony, Auntie Ruth's voice unexpectedly screeched at them like a parrot in a cage.

"You great gorilla! Don't you remember anything? It goes: *I'll grind his bones to make my bread*. You blithering oaf!"

Glancing over her shoulder, Zelie shuddered at the sight of Ruth glaring in her direction.

"Bread," the giant bubbled through slobbery lips, the effort of saying the entire sentence obviously too much for him to manage.

This was it. They were doomed. Zelie knew it now, but she would not make it easy. Ruth and the giant would have to catch her first. Zelie scurried around over the leaves, keeping as far away from the giant as possible. The giant continued the chase.

"Stop doing laps around that ridiculous tree and be quiet, you brainless twerp," Ruth shrieked.

"No," the giant growled, defiantly. "Make my *bread*."

"You've eaten enough, you fat hog! Do something useful."

Suddenly it struck Zelie that Ruth did not understand what the giant was trying to say. She had not spotted them after all. While Zelie, Sawyer and Dresden could see the castle perfectly well from inside the shadows, it must have been dark enough under the leaves to obscure them from Ruth's view. But their presence would not be a secret for long at this rate. Staying out of the giant's way was hard work and the sound of their puffing had snared whatever dull sense of curiosity the giant possessed.

The beanstalk shuddered wildly as he jabbed it from the other side. Zelie toppled off the leaf but caught hold of the edge and held on tight. Meanwhile Sawyer only just managed to save Dresden from falling off the opposite side.

The beanstalk shook again. Clutching the leaf for dear life, Zelie's vision blurred from the vibration.

"What *are* you doing, you oversized baboon? It's dark now. Our queen has given her royal orders," Auntie Ruth squawked as Zelie and Dresden hauled themselves back up onto the leaf and huddled next to Sawyer in the shadows. "You must go and cut the power to the village tonight. Her majesty does not want the children's minds sullied with electronic nonsense from games and televisions. Tomorrow they begin their purification."

The giant snarled belligerently.

"Carry on Monster," Madelene's voice issued from the balcony. Zelie could make out her spooky outline standing beside Ruth. "And while you're in the village, you shall remove the Mayor's bedroom from his house and bring it to me. He shall be busy executing my royal decree. Sleep would be an unnecessary distraction."

The giant gave an acknowledging grunt.

"And get some more food, you greedy bag of lard," Ruth added.

Four huge fingers slapped around the beanstalk, inches below where Zelie perched. Out of the corner of her eye, she saw what looked like a bright blue pebble fall from above, bounce off the giant's wrist and disappear out of sight. The beanstalk trembled and bent under the giant's weight but then swayed upright again as the giant's massive mitt released and rustled out of sight. Hand over clomping hand he thumped downward. The rhythmic rumble was like a slow drum proclaiming the village's impending doom.

# CHAPTER SEVENTEEN

## *Antidote*

As the giant descended to the village, the beanstalk rumbled and the leaves quivered rhythmically for over a minute. Then all fell still. Madelene and Ruth went inside the castle, but the lingering stench left behind by the giant was a haunting reminder of Jack being flung to his doom. How many other people were being hurt right now in the village? How many more houses tossed through the air? And what could Zelie do?

"I can't be here," she murmured, and began to climb.

"Where are you going?" Sawyer called. "What happens when the giant comes back?"

But Zelie did not stop. She had a sudden need to see the stars and be far away from Sawyer's pleading, which faded from hearing as she made her way upwards, leaf by leaf.

The night seemed to be growing brighter as she rose towards the top of the beanstalk and already she felt a little better. Somewhere up there, Jack's star was shining down on her. A soothing blue light pulsed through the foliage. But it was more of a glow than a twinkling. And it seemed almost too close to be starlight. The air even seemed to be growing warmer.

All of a sudden, Zelie realised what the source might be. Excitement bubbled up inside her like fizzy drink poured from a height. And, though she told herself not to hope, she climbed as fast as she could through the shadows towards its eerie glow.

Suddenly bathed in light and warmth, Zelie could not help but gawp at the array of magic bean pods above her, pulsing like Christmas lights under every leaf at the top of the beanstalk. In the misty night air, the beans' orb-like glow made everything seem like a dream. A few of the pods nearby were open and empty. The beans must have fallen out, Zelie thought. Like that blue pebble that bounced off the giant's arm.

She reached out for one of the sausage-sized pods. It was bumpy and black. And pulsing through the slit in its side came that soft blue glow that had mesmerised her a few days earlier. It greeted her fingers with a great surge of brightness as if the pod relished her touch. Its hard, heavy capsule felt like warm metal. It peeled away from the stem easily and opened as if it were hinged on one side. Four glowing ovals lay inside, each with its own unique swirling pattern like the ones she had seen in the garden. Staring at them was as hypnotic as gazing into the dancing flames of a campfire.

*

A yelp from Sawyer far below startled Zelie from her daze. She fell off her perch and landed in the centre of a leaf below, somehow still with the bean pod in hand. There was a frantic scuffle from below and a damp thud, like an orange hitting pavement. Someone yelled an unceremonious "ow" which was followed by Sawyer's loud shushing.

Clutching the bean pod in one hand and moving as quickly and quietly as she could, Zelie climbed downward. Sawyer and Dresden were not where she had left them. A frenetic exchange of whispers sounded out from somewhere below. Down through the leaves she slipped, pausing a moment later to listen. The whispering stopped and there was a deafening pause.

145

"Is that you up there, Squirrel?"

Zelie stiffened. It sounded like Jack's voice. But that was impossible.

"Jack?" she asked, quietly.

"Who else would be daft enough to follow you up here?" said the familiar voice.

It sounded so much like him and she wanted, so much, for it to be true. It seemed so unlikely. Could he have survived? Perhaps it was a trick: one of the witch's nasty incantations. But how could she know to cast such a spell if she did not know Zelie was even there?

Sawyer's voice broke the silence. "Are you coming down or what?" he hissed.

"Just wait a tick, Sawyer," said that familiar voice. "Stillness is no antidote for a curious mind. You'll see."

Zelie lifted the edge of the leaf, cautiously. And by the soft glow of the bean pod, Zelie saw it was true. Against all odds, Jack was alive.

"See, what did I tell you, Sawyer? Curious as a kitten," said Jack.

Zelie's breath caught in her throat and tears sprang to her eyes. "I can't believe it!" she said, almost bowling Jack over as she jumped to embrace him. The cold water from his climb through the cloud seeped from his clothes through hers but she could not care less.

"What are you doing here?"

"Well, there was no sense in staying in the hospital. The doctors couldn't find anything wrong with me. I couldn't go home to my house because, well, it's in pieces and scattered across half of Emerson. I had no doubt that you would be up here in the thick of it and could probably use some help. And I can't turn my back on a lady in need. Because, as you know, there are few men in this world as gallant as Mr Jack Spriggins."

She squeezed him even tighter and he groaned.

"Are you hurt?" Zelie asked, pulling away.

"Here and there. Max makes a rough old dance partner. And Sawyer's little jaw massage didn't help much either."

"You hit him?" Zelie growled at Sawyer.

"I didn't know who it was," Sawyer said in a squeaky voice. "It's dark and he popped up out of nowhere."

"No argument from me, Lad," Jack laughed softly. "I'd have probably done the same. Go easy Squirrel. I'll be fine."

"I thought you had died," Zelie said. "How did you survive?"

"Oh, you're talking about my little tango with Max. Well, it was the funniest thing. When I was falling, I just reached out with this hand and managed to grab on. Mind you, I took down quite a few leaves before I came to a complete stop. I've no idea why, but this hand of mine has the strength of a coyote's jaw since I unwrapped the bandages."

"I think it was something to do with these," Zelie said, smiling. She opened her hand. The blue light shone upwards on Jack and Sawyer making their faces look alien. "Mum poured some concoction on your wounds to heal them. It was made from some magic beans I found in Sawyer's garden."

"Magic beans," nodded Jack. "Didn't think I'd ever see any of those after I chopped down the other beanstalk. Beautiful aren't they? Handy too, if you can work out how to use them. Here, before I forget. Add this little stick of trouble to your tool kit." Jack held the wand out to Zelie. "It's as good to me as teeth to a duck. I'm hoping you've inherited some of your mother's skill with magic."

Sawyer folded his arms and looked off into the

distance.

Zelie took the wand with a sigh of relief. "You're amazing Jack."

"I have my moments. Just keep away from the other end of that wand, alright?"

"I will," Zelie said.

"I'm getting off this beanstalk," said Sawyer, after a dejected glance at the wand.

"Good idea, Sawyer," Jack said. "We want to be well clear before Max comes back. We'll have to find somewhere to hide in the… Oh, he's off." Sawyer seemed to be in a sudden hurry and had already climbed down out of view. "Right then. We'll talk later shall we?"

"Hey Sawyer," called Zelie as she climbed down after him, using the bean pod to light her way. "What's wrong? I thought you'd be happy. Now I have the wand, I can lift that spell from your Auntie."

"I know how to use the wand too, remember?" Sawyer snapped.

Zelie stuffed the wand angrily in her pocket. "Jeez. What's your problem?"

"Nothing!" Sawyer shouted.

"Hey, you two," Jack said, helping Dresden down to the next leaf. "Turn down the volume will you?" But his warning was a little too late.

A moment later, the door of the castle on the other side of the beanstalk clicked and began to whir open. Jack jumped down next to Zelie. They pressed their backs against the trunk of the beanstalk and beckoned Dresden out of sight. But the gnome remained in view of the castle and pointed a finger.

"Auntie R-R-R…" he stammered. There was no need for the second word. Zelie felt the cold crackle over her skin and saw ice crystals begin to form on the leaf around Dresden. Zelie stuffed the bean pod deep into her pocket. The light went out like a candle. Then she lurched forward and pulled Dresden towards her.

As Zelie leaned against the trunk of the beanstalk, her elbow brushed against what felt like a block of ice. Jack's clothes, still damp from his climb up the beanstalk had frozen solid against his skin. Meanwhile the warmth of the bean pod in Zelie's pocket seemed to be dwindling as the ice crept over every nearby surface. Ruth's quick footsteps sounded like they were crunching through snow towards them.

"Who's there!" screeched the rusty wheel of a voice.

Zelie withdrew the wand from her pocket. Sawyer glanced up at it from the leaf below and sneered.

"Who!" Auntie Ruth demanded. "Speak up, or I will wake her highness and she will seek you out in a far less friendly way."

Jack's icy fingers closed around Zelie's as he inhaled a steely breath. "Not a sound," he quivered. The crunching footsteps came closer and the frosted leaves began to curl. Clouds of Zelie's own misty breath threatened to give them away and her teeth chattered until she bit down on her tongue to silence them. She looked at the wand and took a deep breath. This was her moment.

With a sudden jerk, Sawyer reached up and snatched the wand from Zelie's hand. "Over here, Auntie," he called out, leaping out of the shadow. Jack lurched to grab him but his clothes were frozen against the trunk of the beanstalk.

Zelie's trepidation dissolved in her acidic rage. She glared down at Sawyer. The impostor, she thought. All this time, he had just been deceiving her. He had fooled them all into trusting him. How could he? Jack squeezed her hand even tighter and shook his head

149

slowly. The taste of blood was in her mouth where she had bitten down too hard on her tongue. Her muscles pulled like wires under her skin.

"Sawyer?" Auntie Ruth squeaked. "You worthless worm. How did you get all way up here? You must have had help. Who's with you?"

Zelie wanted to leap at Sawyer. To scratch and bite. To lash out with her feet or fists or her hair. Anything.

"I'm alone, Auntie," Sawyer said meekly. "I thought you might need some help."

Zelie frowned at Sawyer standing down there clutching the wand. Anger seeped away into confusion. What was he doing?

"Wonders never cease," Ruth exclaimed. "Well, come on then. Jump down, you imbecile. There's plenty of work to be done."

Zelie heard an icy crunch as Sawyer landed on the snowy cloud. A moment later there was a scuffle and Auntie Ruth's voice, higher and more screeching than usual. "Hey! What are you—Get off, you filthy swine."

Still hidden in the shadow, Zelie turned to a shivering Jack for answers. A blinding flash lit up his baffled face. Zelie's eyes watered and stung and the beanstalk shook with thunder, rattling Jack free of his icy restraints.

"Help," Sawyer screamed. "It's not working—no, Auntie don't—Let go of it!"

Zelie twisted her hand out of Jack's grip and hopped out of the shadows. There was Sawyer wrestling with Auntie Ruth in a mound of snow, both of them clutching at the wand. Flames flickered from Ruth's shoulder where the lightning bolt must have hit. Sawyer had tried to lift her spell using only the wand and it had backfired yet again. Ruth had almost pried the wand from his fingers.

Without thinking, Zelie ran and jumped as far as she could into the cold air ignoring the sharp bite of the whistling wind and the sting of the freezing snow as she landed and rolled onto the cloud. And before she really knew what she was doing, she scooped up a snowball and threw it at Auntie Ruth. In his struggle, Sawyer moved into its path. But at the last moment, Ruth yanked him sideways and the snowball exploded onto her scowling face. Sawyer pulled the wand from her grasp and pinned her to the ground, his hands blue with cold.

"Do something," he cried.

Zelie pushed as quickly as she could through the deep snow to Sawyer and opened his backpack. Zelie's fingers found Sawyer's drink bottle and pulled it free of the bag. The slosh of unfrozen water felt like a small victory in itself. She reached over Sawyer, snatched the wand and held it against the bottle with one hand while the numb fingers of her other hand fumbled the lid open.

Auntie Ruth spat out the remains of the snowball. "Let me go, you vermin!" she grunted, spraying spittle into the air that fell as ice crystals on her face and clothes. "My Queen! Wake up! Wake up!"

Into the bottle went a bean from Zelie's pocket. She clapped her hand over the opening and shook it, madly. What was that spell?

"By the power of this wand and the magic of this bean…" she began.

Hearing these words, Ruth thrashed and bucked underneath Sawyer like a roped bull.

"Break this curse's bond… and let nature… um,"

With a jolting voice, Sawyer managed to speak the last word of the spell. "Su—per—vene."

"Supervene," Zelie repeated.

One of the shards dissolved from the wand and a bright flash shone inside the drink bottle. For the briefest moment, Zelie saw the bones of her hand and, with a gasp, she withdrew it from the opening. Purple mist puffed from the bottle and Ruth thrashed even more furiously as Zelie poured its contents over her face and chest. Thick hot steam rose up from Auntie Ruth's body. Sawyer stood up and emerged backwards out of the steam, cupping his hands over his mouth and nose.

The steam cleared and Ruth remained lying on her back. She was completely still, eyes open, body rigid and a face like barbed wire. The concoction seemed to have merely paralysed her and dissolved some of the cloud beneath her head.

Zelie was certain Madelene would have woken up with all the commotion. She shot a nervous glance at the castle. But to her relief and surprise, all was quiet and dark.

Sawyer made a little excited squeak, restoring Zelie's attention. Ruth's cruel puckered face had begun to relax and a healthy pink glow eased under her pale skin. Her eyes fluttered as if waking from a trance and a look of distress and confusion came over her. But then her eyes met Sawyer's and she leapt to her feet. And before Sawyer could step away, she wrapped him in a tight embrace, whispering something in his ear that brought a smile to his lips and a glisten to his eyes.

"It's alright Auntie," he sniffed. "It's not your fault."

As great tears of happiness streamed down Sawyer's cheeks, Zelie felt a quiet swell of pride. Smiling, she put the lid on the remaining concoction and bent down to put it away in her backpack.

She was about to zip up the bag when she happened to notice that an oddly shaped pit had formed where the excess concoction had washed over

Ruth. It was lined with a clear gel-like coating. And because Zelie felt a little uncomfortable watching Ruth and Sawyer gushing over each other, she poked at it with the wand for something to do.

As she prodded more and more, the gel began to peel away at the edges of the hole. And when she pulled on it with her fingers, it lifted free in one piece. Its shape resembled a jester's hat. What a perfect substitute crown it would make for Madelene, Zelie thought. But the gel would not hold its form. It was soft, like a cross between Plasticine and Play Doh, but colourless and extremely light. It might make a half-decent pillow if they had to stay up here for another night. She decided to keep it.

Zelie stuffed the gel into her bag alongside the remains of the gnomes. And as she did, one of the broken pieces of terracotta flipped over to reveal a painted eye and part of a furrowed brow. It was Thurin, looking up at her, as if pleading for help. For a moment, Zelie thought about using the wand to reassemble the gnomes right there and then, but something about Sawyer's inability to use the wand earlier made her hesitate.

"Not yet, gnomes," she whispered. "Not yet."

Zelie glanced again at the balcony. There was still no sign of Madelene but the sky had begun to brighten and a blanket of higher cloud on the horizon was showing a hint of orange. It was almost morning. The giant would return soon and Madelene would be up looking for Ruth to perform some sort of chore. She looked over to Sawyer and Ruth who were still hugging. Hurry up, she thought.

"Aye aye. There's a familiar face," came Jack's jolly voice from a leaf just above Ruth's head. Zelie felt relieved. Surely he would get them moving.

Dresden was wedged beneath one of Jack's arms looking thoroughly indignant.

"Hello my little garden friend," cried Ruth. "And Jack, it's so lovely to see you."

Jack leapt from the beanstalk and landed knee deep in the snow, setting Dresden down beside him.

"Well, I see you have lost none of your youthful energy, Jack," said Ruth.

"My pumpkin soup is the secret. At least two bowls a day. Delicious," said Jack, showing none of the urgency Zelie had hoped for.

"Ooh, can I have your recipe?"

Zelie foresaw another lengthy reunion. "I'm really sorry to interrupt, but didn't we agree to stay out of sight?" Zelie whispered, checking the castle balcony for the third time.

"Right you are," said Jack.

"We don't need to hide any more," said Sawyer. "Auntie can undo the curse right now, can't you Auntie? Please hurry. I want to go home."

But of course, Zelie thought. Sawyer was right. In Ruth's hands, the wand's power would match Madelene's magic. They had been counting on it. Zelie felt a surge of excitement. Clear skies and freedom, not just today, but always. It was a dream come true. She held up the wand for Ruth to take.

"I have some magic beans as well if you need them," said Zelie.

Ruth frowned at the wand. "I'm afraid that won't work," she said. "I'm sorry, Dear. I don't know how to cast that spell in an unselfish way."

"But Auntie," Sawyer said, quietly. "Didn't you use it on the witch before? Jack said you cast her out to sea."

"Well yes," Ruth said. "But Madelene had just put a spell on me. I didn't know it was a curse at the time. I was sure I was dying. It was painful and slow. But all I could think about was you, Sawyer, and how terrible it would be if you became a slave to Madelene. I had to save you. I had to be sure you would be OK, even if I wasn't alive to look after you. It's different now. I'm not dying. I'm not even cursed, thanks to this lovely young lady. If the cloud were gone, I'd be much better off, just like everyone else."

A fearful chill crept up Zelie's spine. What were they supposed to do now?

# CHAPTER EIGHTEEN

## *Time's Up*

The layer of snow on the surface of the cloud made it almost impossible for little Dresden to walk towards the castle. So Zelie went over and put him on her shoulders then trudged after Ruth, who apparently knew a good place to hide. Sawyer waited and then fell in step beside Zelie.

"Thank you so much for changing Auntie back to the way she was," Sawyer said. "I should have let you do it in the first place."

"That's all right."

"I just really thought the wand was going to work for me this time," Sawyer said. "I mean, it did before, right? I put you in that worm tunnel."

"Yeah. That was pretty cool," Zelie said. "Do you want it back?"

"No," Sawyer said, with a regretful sigh. "I think you better keep it for now. Just in case I set it off again."

"Sure," Zelie said, trying not to sound too relieved.

"When we get to where Auntie is taking us, maybe you could use it to repair the other gnomes."

"Yeah," Zelie said with a frown. "That should be pretty simple, shouldn't it?"

"Not for me. But maybe I'm more selfish than you," Sawyer said. After an awkward pause he gave Dresden's foot a friendly squeeze. "You're going to get your friends back, little man. Then maybe you can tell us what you were trying to say earlier?"

Dresden nodded vigorously. Perhaps he knew one of Madelene's weaknesses, Zelie thought then gasped as the wand vibrated fiercely in her hand.

"What was that?" Sawyer said.

"The wand," Zelie said. "It just sort of… buzzed."

"Whoah, be careful," Sawyer said. "That happened to me just before I tried to clean the pigs."

"That's weird," said Zelie.

As dawn bloomed, the snow began to melt. Zelie was happy for the return of some sensation to the tips of her toes, but the thawing cloud began to stretch like an elastic mat making it increasingly difficult to walk. Ruth had no such trouble, though Zelie noticed that she walked in quite an unnatural way.

Once the snow had melted completely, Zelie had to use all her focus just to avoid falling over. The cloud felt soft underfoot. But a second after every step, it rebounded violently. It reminded Zelie of a game she used to play with her friends on school camps. She had to stand for as long as possible on the top bunk while one of her friends was below kicking as hard as they could at the underside of the mattress. She would never last more than twenty seconds before falling into a giggling heap. Walking over the cloud was even more difficult than that and nowhere near as fun. Despite intense concentration, Zelie was a stumbling tangle of flailing feet and buckling knees. In her struggle, Dresden toppled from her shoulders and began to make his own way. His tiny footsteps made no impression on the elastic cloud. He wafted past the stragglers and stood proudly next to Ruth who had paused beside the castle and was now rising and falling gently on the ripples made by the heavier footsteps of her followers.

The wisps of clouds on the horizon were now a deep orange and the sky above had turned from deep purple to pale blue. A bright yellow glint shone on the tips of the castle's spires, high in the sky. For Zelie, it was the briefest of glimpses as she struggled over the cloud. But by the time she caught up with Ruth, a bright crest of light had appeared on the horizon, lifting the heavy frown of concentration from her face.

"We're not out of harm's way yet, my pet. We have to reach the roof," Ruth said, beckoning Zelie away from the view. Zelie wanted to protest but thought better of it. She permitted herself one last yearning gaze at the blooming sunrise, lingering until she feared she might be left behind. She stepped into the shadow of the castle with a shudder that came more from resentment than the drop in temperature. A moment later, her feet were ejected from the cloud and she found herself staring up at the sky.

Before rising to her feet, Zelie paused a moment to watch Ruth. Perhaps she was walking in that strange way on purpose. It was certainly more effective than anyone else. While Jack and Sawyer were jerking about as if a cruel puppeteer had control of their limbs, Ruth's shuffling feet produced almost no reaction from the cloud. When Zelie got carefully to her feet and mimicked the technique, she found that a shorter, faster stride had a flattening effect on the bumps and ripples and she overtook the others quickly. By the time they reached the barn, the whole group had caught on and shifted into a similar waddle. They must have looked like a parade of penguins. Luckily, there was no one around to see.

"We must get out of sight before the giant arrives back from the village—especially you Jack," Ruth said, nodding at him as she rounded the rear corner of the castle. "His mind might work poorly, but he does not forget an order."

Zelie cast her mind back. The last time Madelene had issued an order to the giant about Jack, it was to throw him down through the hole in the cloud.

Ruth pointed towards the roof of the castle. It was the height of a five floor building. "There's a door on the other side of that parapet," she said, pointing to where rectangular gaps appeared at intervals along the top of the wall.

"It's a pretty big climb," Zelie observed.

"Well, Dear, compared to scaling that beanstalk, reaching that roof will be a doddle," said Ruth. And she began an excruciatingly slow ascent up the rear corner of the castle. A line formed beneath her and Zelie found herself at the end of it. She thought about using the wand to lift them all up onto the roof. There might still be time to catch the last of the sunrise.

The wand buzzed in her hand again.

"Hey," said Sawyer. "Point that thing away from me. It sounds like it's about to go off."

He was right, of course. That would have been a fairly selfish way to use the wand. But why did it vibrate earlier when she thought about fixing the gnomes? And then it struck her. At the time, Sawyer was suggesting that Dresden might be able to reveal some sort of advantage over Madelene. Was that all it took to make it a selfish spell?

Buzz, went the wand, as if to answer her question.

Zelie's surprise gave way to confusion. She had intended to put the gnomes back together long before Sawyer mentioned any benefit. That should count for something, she thought.

Buzz-buzz, threatened the wand. Apparently it did not matter at all.

She clenched her jaw tight to stop the scream from escaping and glared at the wand, finally understanding

159

Sawyer's earlier frustration with it. She had an urge to break it over her knee but instead she thrust it angrily into her pocket and shook her head. After all their plans to get the wand, now it seemed they could not even use it for the simplest of spells. And now all they could do was hide like rats in a sewer.

To Zelie, it seemed to be taking ages for Ruth to climb the castle wall. In truth, it had taken less than a minute for her to reach roughly halfway. Dresden and Jack were already on the wall and Sawyer was waiting his turn but it was not fast enough. She was missing the sunrise. Zelie tried to tell herself to be patient—that there would be another time—but even as she did, her eyes were scanning for a better way up. As Sawyer lifted himself onto the wall, a small ripple expanded from where his foot left the cloud and it gave Zelie an idea.

After a quick glance at the parapet, she waddled forward and gave a small hop into the air to make a wave. Then she jumped hard with both feet just ahead of the wave she had just made. The cloud rebounded with a force that almost dragged the skin off her face. An involuntary scream escaped her lips as she sailed past the climbers. But as she soared into the sky above the castle, the brightness of the sun forced her eyes closed and she lost her bearings.

"Take me to the parapet," she called urgently and was immediately pulled downwards by her hair. She landed hard on the stone roof, adding another bruise to her collection. There was a muttering of varied emotions from the climbers on the other side of the parapet, but Zelie barely heard them. She pulled herself upright to take in the sight.

The sun's red forehead peeked across the cloud, warming her cool skin. A vast ball of beauty, it seemed to float out of the horizon, spraying wisps of higher clouds with a celebration of colours that seemed even more beautiful than at sunset. In her daze, she was only vaguely aware of the others arriving, one-by-one, onto the rooftop. Another minute past as more of the sun became visible, morphing from red to golden and then bright yellow. Its warmth spread through her, just as the beans had that first time in the garden. Zelie stared until her stinging eyes were slits and tears flooded her cheeks. Finally, the sun became too bright and she had to turn her back.

As she wiped the tears from her eyes, she was greeted with a new spectacle. Shadows longer than any she had ever seen stretched out over the cloud surface like stick figures. She waved her arms and giggled as one of the shadows danced along with her movements.

"Well that's the hard part," said Ruth, as Dresden pulled on Sawyer's sleeve to help him through the gap in the parapet. "Now follow me inside and tread softly now." Ruth walked along a platform of uneven stones towards a wooden door.

"Oh dear," said Ruth, clanking at the handle on the door. "I must have locked it from the inside."

Zelie made her way across the stones, intending to open the door with the power of her hair. She was halfway there when, out of the corner of her eye, she spotted movement in the shadow of the beanstalk. Its topmost leaves were shaking in a slow rhythm. A moment later, the outline of the giant emerged lazily from the hole in the cloud and loped towards the castle.

She tiptoed the rest of the way across the roof to where Sawyer was attempting to open the door. Here, she was hidden from the giant by one of the castle's towers.

"The giant's here," she said softly.

Sawyer gasped and Jack stepped just clear of the

shadow of the castle tower to steal a glance. "We'd better get a wriggle on."

"Let me open the door," Zelie said.

"Good idea, Squirrel," said Jack, beckoning Sawyer out of the way. "Watch this Ruth. You're in for a treat."

"Hair," began Zelie. A chime rang out. But before she could issue an instruction, the giant's head and shoulders appeared right beside the castle, his chest level with the ledge. It was Ruth's turn to gasp this time, while Sawyer flattened himself against the stone wall.

The giant's glassy eyed stare froze Zelie to the spot. Though he had shrunk to roughly half size again, Zelie could not stop quivering with fear. But his gaze remained blank and failed to show even the slightest concern. Instead, he looked at her the way a lion might look at a lettuce leaf. Apparently, it did not register that there was a girl atop his master's castle trying to break in. After the giant rounded the rear corner of the castle, his empty gaze shifted to Sawyer then to Dresden and then Ruth as he lumbered towards the barn. From his back hung a huge hessian sack. Jutting from its folds were the roots of at least four upturned fruit trees, two live cows—which mooed over the giant's shoulder— and a wooden stable with the horse still inside it. When he reached the opposite side the castle, his lazy stare rolled to Jack.

The giant's face hardened into a frightening grimace. With a growl, the hessian bag dropped from his back. And in one swift and smelly movement, he reached down and plucked Jack off the roof like a salt shaker off a dining table. His shrunken hand was barely big enough to wrap around Jack's body, though it was certainly still capable of crushing him.

Zelie ran towards the giant. She had to free Jack from the giant's grasp quickly. A bolt of lightning should

162

be enough, she thought and pulled the wand from her pocket. "Stay clear," she called to Dresden, whose pattering footsteps were approaching from behind. She held up the wand, taking great care to make sure the other end was not pointed at anyone behind her. But before Zelie could think of something selfish to wish for, Jack spoke.

"Listen to me," he laboured. "You're not a monster. You're my brother. Do you hear me? Your name is Max."

Instead of hurrying away to dispatch Jack back down the hole as Ruth had suggested he might, the giant became motionless. His thick brow hung heavily over dark glaring eyes fixed on Jack. His greasy hair was matted in dirty clumps on his head. Hunks of pink meat and dried drool wafted on breezy breaths in his bristly beard. Slowly, the giant's frown softened. He scratched his head with a sound like a rake being drawn over gravel.

"Can you remember?" prompted Jack. "Brother?"

The morning light twinkled in the giant's eyes, the corners of his mouth moved upwards in what vaguely resembled a smile and he drew in a breath. "BA-BAAAH!" he bellowed in loud recognition. "BA-BAAAH!"

The moist stench from the giant's outburst blew at Zelie like a hurricane gust, coating her skin and burning her nostrils. Dresden fanned the smell of the giant's breath away from his grimacing face.

"Ruth!" the haunting voice of Madelene echoed from inside the walls of the castle. "Dawn has come and gone. You're late! Why is the monster repeating an incoherent syllable instead of standing beside my window waiting for his spell?"

Zelie swung around. Ruth was shaking her head rapidly, eyes wide with a hand over her mouth.

"Ruth, answer me!" ordered Madelene.

In desperation, Ruth gripped at her throat and squeezed. "A thousand apologies, my Queen," she screeched in a voice so very close to the cursed one she had recently surrendered.

"That's better," said Madelene, apparently fooled. "Now, tell me. Did my monster bring me the Mayor's bedroom as I ordered?"

Ruth glanced over the parapet at the spilled contents of the giant's hessian sack. "He appears to have brought a horse's stable instead," she said.

Madelene groaned and something inside the castle smashed. "Hopeless! I said the Mayor's bedroom, not a mare's. What does a queen have to do to get good help? Sit in your spot, Monster, and keep quiet. You'll be lucky if I don't have you made into meat loaf and fed to the children when they arrive." The giant slinked to the back corner of the castle and sat down against it, causing the castle to rumble. Then he sat staring at Jack as if he were a china doll.

The cows and the horse had found their way free of the hessian bag and began crunching on the apples from the upturned fruit trees.

"What is that noise?" Madelene's head appeared out of the window of the castle and Zelie had to flatten herself against the parapet to stay out of sight. She pulled Dresden beside her and held her breath. "Please don't notice Jack," she said, quietly. If Madelene saw him in the giant's grasp, there was no way she would let him survive again. But she seemed flustered and preoccupied.

"Ruth!"

"Yes Highness," said Ruth, shuffling over to hide Zelie. She had adopted a hunched posture with some of her hair pulled over her face to obscure it.

"What are you going to do about that mess?"

"I'll get to it right away, Majesty."

"Right, good—No, don't. Not yet, anyway. There isn't time," Madelene said, sounding anxious and rushed. "It has been twenty-four hours since I gave my orders. I expect my servants will be waiting. A queen must be punctual."

"Yes Queen."

"And for once, I expect you shall maintain order over the monster while I present myself to the villagers."

"Yes Queen," Ruth said. Her voice was becoming more of a squeak than a screech. But Madelene seemed unaware.

"So help me, Ruth, if that monster causes any trouble, I will empty every vial on my belt. I'll cast spells that will make your nightmares seem like fairytales. Do you understand me?"

"Yes Queen."

And with that, Madelene disappeared inside the window.

Zelie had no time to congratulate Ruth on such a fine impression of her former self because only a few seconds later, Madelene's echoing voice rang out from the direction of the balcony. She called out in rhyme:

"Oh cursed cloud now follow my hand.

Raise, spin and lower on my command."

The castle sank away beneath Zelie's feet so fast that she and her companions hung in the air above it. From her slightly elevated position, Zelie could see over the battlements. Madelene was standing on the balcony reading from a very large book that lay open on an ornate metal stand. She seemed to be doing an elaborate mime. It looked almost as if she were using the very tip of her finger to press a very long, but apparently invisible, broom handle into a deep hole.

Beyond her, the beanstalk appeared to be shooting upwards through the cloud at an incredible pace, becoming thicker and darker as it ascended.

In fact, the beanstalk was not moving at all. Madelene was using her hand to direct the cloud to fall down through the air. Zelie's feet had barely caught up with the castle roof when the pace of the cloud's fall slowed and gravity seemed to double. Ruth crumbled to the ground but Sawyer, Dresden and Zelie managed to keep their feet. The whole castle dipped into the cloud, like a boulder on a trampoline. Then it rebounded up, crashing like a cutlery drawer sending everyone to their hands and knees or onto their backs. Finally the cloud came to rest.

Zelie had bumped her knee as she landed. The groans from Ruth and Sawyer told her that they had suffered similar wounds but, thankfully, nobody seemed to be hurt too badly. Even Dresden's terracotta body had survived the fall, having only grazed the faded paint from one of his elbows.

Zelie limped as quickly as she could to the front of the castle, followed closely by Sawyer and Ruth, and peered over the wall.

Madelene seemed to be in no mood for delay. Facing the beanstalk, she uncorked a vial of green liquid from her belt and muttered an impatient verse from the large book on the metal stand:

"So that queen and kin may see,
Pry up this patch of cloud for me."

The liquid began to smoke and bubble. With a flourish, Madelene emptied the vial onto the cloud and performed some sort of grasping action in the air with the other hand. A deafening tearing sound brought Zelie's hands to her ears. To her astonishment, a section of cloud was peeling back like the lid from a tin of beans leaving a crescent-shaped hole in the cloud that extended from the beanstalk and all the way around the far side of the castle.

The sun shining through the new hole in the cloud made the village resemble a brightly coloured painting of devastation. It was both beautiful and terrible at the same time. Zelie recognised the remains of Ruth's garden directly below, which looked to have been cleared of most of its rubble and now shone in various shades of green and brown. Chocolate coloured water had pooled in the indentations of the giant's footprints. The nearby terrace houses were so smashed up now that their variously shaded components looked like a mixture of potpourri and toothpicks had been scattered across the ground. A layer of frost had settled over the top of the ruins which glittered in the sunlight. Undamaged neighbouring houses lurked in the grey shade. Their rooftops were only a few feet away from touching the underside of the cloud.

Madelene twisted an emerald ring on one of her fingers and cupped her hands to her mouth. Her voice rang out as if it were on a loudspeaker. "Mayor Andrews, you incompetent fool! How dare you cause your queen to wait."

A tubby short man appeared from the shadows, half squinting, half smiling. His thin hair was slicked to the side and he wore a grey suit and a purple cravat. "I am here, ah, your majesty. Oh look, the sun. How lovely."

"I see no children assembled here, Mr Mayor. Have you lost the ability to read the time or perhaps every clock in the village has malfunctioned?"

"Well, you see," he said, lacing his fingers. "Some of the parents had a little trouble with the idea of giving up their little ones. So I have come to ask if you would, ah, reconsider. Perhaps we can negotiate a solution agreeable for all."

"This is non-compliance, Douglas. You leave me no choice," Madelene said, raising her hand like a pincer. She closed the gap between her fingers and thumb slowly. The cloud responded by inching towards the ground. The houses and buildings beneath the cloud splintered, crunched and crumbled while their residents cried out in horror. Then Madelene slowly twisted her wrist. The cloud—and everything on it—moved in a slow revolution around the beanstalk, sheering the roofs of all the houses away from their walls and collapsing the few panels of the twisted fence that remained. The rotation of the cloud gave Zelie a heart-wrenching glimpse inside the roofless houses.

Families scrambled to huddle in the corners and crawled under tables and beds for safety from the descending spinning cloud. When the castle had turned roughly halfway around the beanstalk, Madelene held up her palm and widened her fingers. The cloud stopped spinning and rose upwards above the fresh destruction.

From this new position Zelie could see the shoreline through the hole in the cloud. The park was no longer a tranquil open space but a jumble of broken roofs, tiles and timbers that had been pulled off the houses and then rolled underneath the low cloud towards the sea.

Madelene smoothed her hair and gown and then twisted the ring on her finger again.

"Mr Mayor. Your queen awaits your presence in the park. Come immediately."

A minute later, Mayor Andrews appeared from the direction of the village, his suit torn and covered in dust, his ingratiating smile replaced by a pained grimace. Holding his hip, he limped over the rubble into the sunlight beneath the hole.

"Please, your Highness. No more."

"I expect I have your full attention now, Douglas."

"Yes, Majesty. Thank you. A fine lesson in, ah, humility."

"Indeed," said Madelene, lifting her nose in the air. "Now, I shall have what's mine. Bring me my children."

"Majesty, I imagine that, after your fine demonstration, the parents are, right now, pondering the wisdom of obedience. But, with the village in a state of, ah, disrepair, would you please grant us another day to make the arrangements?"

"I will grant you two hours," Madelene said brusquely, then calmed herself by drawing another circle with her nose. "If you fail to assemble the children by then, I shall conjure a monsoon over your village with rains more severe than you would ever dare imagine. Without a single roof to offer shelter or any boats to provide escape, the consequences may be somewhat distressing. Especially so for the parents, I speculate. Unless, of course, the children have all learned to swim?"

Mayor Andrews made to speak but Madelene had already made a rude-looking upward gesture with her finger. The cloud and castle rocketed back up into the sky leaving the ruined village far below in the shadows.

# CHAPTER NINETEEN

## *Is a Trickle Enough?*

It sickened Zelie to look at Madelene now. All these years, she had deprived the village of the sun and the stars. She had torn the roofs from the houses and now she would drown everyone unless they gave away their children. Her obsession with power was grotesque. And there was no guarantee, nor even a suggestion, that she would remove the curse of the cloud even if she were made queen.

The drizzly grey of the village seemed as if it would be unbearable now. How could anyone live like that when a sky like this was possible? She finally understood why the adults longed for clear skies and warmth. Zelie glowered at Madelene as she revelled in the stolen sunshine, stretching her delicate neck and giving off tiny coughs as if she were too elegant to properly clear her throat.

"Ruth," barked Madelene once the cloud had risen to full height. "Ruth!" she shouted again, even more impatiently, as she turned towards Zelie who ducked out of sight. "Oh there you are Ruth. You must speak when I summon."

Ruth remained frozen. Her face was a picture of shock.

"I have only a few vials remaining on my belt," said Madelene. "And I have depleted my supply of magic beans in the castle. You will go to the beanstalk and bring me two of the ripest pods you can find. Then you may spend the remainder of the morning remediating that mess." She gestured in the direction of the hessian bag that the giant had brought up from the village.

Ruth remained silent and still.

"Well?" said Madelene.

Ruth swallowed thickly and nodded obediently as if she could not find the words. Then she retreated out of sight while Madelene slapped herself on the thigh and promised never again to rush an important curse.

Zelie rushed to the back corner of the castle and peered quietly over the top, blocking her nose from the stench rising off the giant. Jack was barely visible inside the loose grip of one of his fat fingered hands and, despite all the commotion, somehow the brothers had fallen asleep. They both must have been exhausted after being awake for most of last night.

"What now?" whispered Sawyer, appearing at her side, followed by Ruth and Dresden. "Should we still hide?"

"No, we have to stop that *witch*," Zelie said. The word 'witch' erupted like poison gas from between her clenched teeth.

"That may, in fact, be possible," Ruth said, excitedly. "Madelene has left herself vulnerable. She has used up most of her magic. I'm convinced our very best chance now will be to obtain her book of spells and harvest every single one of those beans from the beanstalk. Madelene cannot perform her spells without them. The fate of the entire village now depends on us."

Dresden seemed to agree because he started pointing at Ruth as if she had spoken the very words he was trying to convey all along.

"But first we have to rescue Jack," Zelie said. "We could climb down to the giant and-"

Sawyer interjected with a series of squeaks that even

had Ruth looking concerned.

"I believe what Sawyer is trying to say," Ruth said, peering over the edge. "Is that it's likely Max will wake up if you disturb him."

"I have some concoction left over," Zelie said withdrawing Sawyer's bottle. "It's only a trickle though. Is that going to be enough?"

"I really don't know, Dear. You seem to have the impression that I know all there is to understand about magic. But I was only learning myself when Madelene and I had a difference of opinion about how magic should be used. The one thing I do know is that magic beans are essential. So we must go."

"No. I won't leave Jack here like that. No way," Zelie said, firmly. "I'll have to use what's left in the bottle." Zelie pulled out the wand and tested the idea by picturing the giant as a smaller version of Jack. This time, the wand did not buzz. "OK. I think it's going to work," she said with a nod. She leaned out and carefully trickled the remaining liquid onto the giant's head while she quietly spoke the words of the rhyme.

"By the power of this wand and the magic of this bean…"

The giant snorted causing Sawyer to cower behind Zelie's knees.

Zelie tried to slow the flow from the bottle but there were only drips remaining now. The last part of her spell was so rushed that some of the words ran together. "Break this curse's bond-and-let-nature-supervene."

To Zelie's dismay, apart from having slightly damp hair, the giant looked completely unaffected.

"It didn't work. I need to make some more concoction. Do you have any more water Sawyer?"

Sawyer shook his head. "I only brought that one bottle."

"There's a well inside the castle," offered Ruth. "But we have no time. If we delay any longer, we risk leaving some of those magic beans behind."

"But," Zelie said, "Jack would never leave me like this. Never. And if the giant wakes up and that *witch* orders him to…" Suddenly she had an idea. "Wait, what if the giant couldn't hear any of her commands?" Out of her backpack, Zelie withdrew the gel she had peeled from the pit in the cloud. She tore it in half and rolled it into two equal sized balls. "What if we put this stuff in his ears?"

"Ear plugs? A splendid idea," Ruth said. "But I fear we still risk waking him up."

"Me!" boomed Dresden, even shocking himself with how loudly he had spoken.

The giant chowed a few times on an invisible morsel of food but remained asleep.

"Please… I… do it," struggled Dresden in a much quieter voice.

Zelie nodded. She could not trust her hair to place the ear plugs without waking the giant. But Dresden was small enough to get the job done and light enough to be lowered on Sawyer's rope, which Sawyer was only too happy to tie in a neat knot around Dresden's waist.

"Please be careful," encouraged Zelie, as he leaned off the side of the wall. "And just to be safe, you'd better keep your mouth shut, alright?"

As smoothly as she could, Zelie lowered Dresden towards the giant's shoulder, remaining poised to pull him to safety. But she had no need for worry. Dresden placed both wads of gel without so much as a twitch from the giant.

"Oh, well done, little fellow," said Ruth, as Zelie hoisted Dresden back onto the castle roof. "Now we must all make great haste. There is less than two hours now to harvest all those beans. And the clock is ticking."

Zelie rushed across the roof and ordered the castle door open. A tendril of her hair wormed inside the keyhole and sprang the lock. Zelie had expected the door to be torn from its hinges but after Ruth lavished her with astonishing praise for her intelligence and subtlety, she could hardly tell her the truth. Inside the door was not a small room, as Zelie expected, but a spiral staircase leading down to a lower level of the castle.

"I will get the spell book," Ruth said. "I know my way around the castle."

"I'll help," said Sawyer, grabbing Ruth's hand.

"No Sawyer. Zelie and this little gnome will need your help. Be brave now child."

Sawyer hesitated, then buried his fists in his pockets and nodded, dutifully. "OK Auntie."

"Can you please get some water from the well?" Zelie asked, holding out Sawyer's empty drink bottle to Ruth. "We'll need some more concoction to save Jack."

"I will try," said Ruth. She took the bottle and shrugged off her shawl. "And you better take this with you. In case Madelene happens to look for me on the beanstalk," she explained. The shawl was not much of a disguise but it was better than nothing, Zelie supposed.

"You three must get every single bean. You understand?" said Ruth. "There are many more than you might expect. And you will have to hurry now. Madelene is rarely late, so you must finish before the two hours is up. I'll meet you at the beanstalk. Now hurry, my cherubs. And good luck." And with that, she pattered down the stairs and out of sight.

*

Dresden seemed to understand the urgency of the situation and began to climb down the corner wall of the castle. With brief relish, Zelie considered jumping off the side and allowing the cloud to cushion her fall. She quickly dismissed the thought. Even the smallest ripple might wake the giant. So she followed Dresden, half expecting Sawyer to follow Ruth inside the castle. But he was true to his word and after a brief moment, she saw him lower himself from the parapet above Zelie.

When she was roughly half way down, she heard Dresden slip. A loose stone fell from the wall and cracked loudly against a small ledge further down. Thank goodness for those ear plugs, Zelie thought. But even as she was thinking this, a booming voice rang out from below.

"Don't want to do breaking," it mumbled, solemnly.

"Dresden!" she hissed, giving him the most fiery glare she could muster.

The gnome shook his head and pointed towards the giant. The uneven stones of the wall were obstructing Zelie's view. All she could see was the giant's foot on the end of his twitching leg at the base of the castle. Had it shrunk? It was still big for a human but nothing like the huge wrecking ball-sized feet that had chased them through the streets. The giant seemed to be having a vivid dream.

"You're no queen!" he shouted, kicking out the foot. Then he mumbled: "silly witch."

Zelie climbed down the wall as quickly as she could, overtaking Dresden. She was certain now that the leg was becoming shorter, even as she descended and she did not want to miss the end of the transformation. Stepping carefully onto the cloud, she told herself to stay cautious and withdrew the wand

175

from her back pocket. To her relief, Jack was unharmed. As she shuffled over, Jack rolled his body from the giant's shrinking grasp.

The ship's sail that the giant was using in place of clothes looked enormous now. It had been wrapped so tightly around the giant when he was at his biggest. Now it lay about his body in a crumpled pile. Jack crawled across it to the cloud on the far side and then turned and drew the back of his hand across his forehead to wipe away the sweat. The concoction's effect had been delayed. And though it was obviously still in the process of shrinking the giant, he was still enormous next to Jack who, instead of fleeing, remained right next to the giant, clasping his hands and grinning as if he were doting over a new puppy.

"No. Too much meat," the giant suddenly muttered in his sleep and burped loudly. Jack stifled a laugh.

"What are you doing, Jack?" Zelie whispered, without taking her eyes off the giant.

Jack waved Zelie closer. "I'm getting my bro back."

She doubted the wisdom of staying, but Jack seemed completely unconcerned and Zelie was excited to witness the results of another successful spell. She paced a wide arc around the sleeping giant to where Jack stood. By the time she arrived at his side, the giant had stopped shrinking altogether.

"Now I know how the gnomes feel when they stand next to us," Zelie said. She guessed the giant was roughly three times bigger than Jack now and his skin on his face and shoulders was smooth and hairless. All the dried up food and other various substances that had been trapped in his beard were now heaped in a disgusting pile on his lap.

"Max?" Sawyer whispered, appearing behind Zelie. He sounded more intrigued, than frightened. Zelie was too, though she feared this was only a temporary transformation for the giant.

"Of course it's Max," Jack answered, showing no concern at all.

"Let's see if he knows that," said Zelie. She nudged the giant's outstretched foot with the wand and quickly stepped back what she thought would be a safe distance.

The giant's heavy breathing stopped abruptly. He blinked and straightened his neck. "Hello," he said, cheerfully.

"Who are you?" Zelie demanded.

"Fine thank you—Argh! I'm so loud inside my brain," he said, shaking his head so wildly that Zelie almost unleashed a bolt of lightning at him. The giant rubbed at his ears, dislodging the ear plugs which bounced off in opposite directions. "Ah, yes, better now," he said with a smile. "And how are you?"

"Not *how* are you! I said *who* are you?"

"Oh, my name is Monster. No, wait, that's not right. Er, it's—Max," he said, finally as if recalling a hazy memory.

"That's right," Jack laughed. He put his hand on Max's big toe and shook it affectionately. Max giggled.

Zelie lowered the wand.

"Yes, Max is my name," Max repeated with a smile. "And who are you?" he said with mock aggression, imitating Zelie. Then he laughed at himself. "Shake hands?"

"Get back!" Zelie shouted.

The giant had extended his huge hand in greeting but recoiled with a gasp as Zelie threatened him again with the wand. "Please little witch. You not use that on me, OK?"

Jack placed his hand on the wand. "There'll be no

177

need for that, Squirrel. Max isn't going to hurt anyone."

"Thank you Mister," said Max.

"Who are you calling Mister? Don't you recognise your own brother?" Jack said.

Max's eyebrows shot up in recognition. "Wait. Ha, yes, my brother. You were the big one and I was the little one."

"That's right bro!" exclaimed Jack.

"The one who hugs me like this." Max gathered Jack into his arms and beat him affectionately on the back. "Ha ha. Like a drum. Ha ha."

"Easy feller," Jack said between thumps. "You don't… know… your strength."

Max lifted him by his waist and placed him back next to Zelie as if he weighed nothing. His smile took up his whole face. But, despite his sweet charm, Zelie felt it was only a matter of time before it all went sour.

*

"Are you daft girl?" exclaimed Jack after hearing Zelie tell him the plan. "You ought to have skedaddled off this cloud when you had a chance."

"I couldn't leave you though," Zelie said.

"Max and I can look after each other. What made you let Ruth go cavorting through the castle on her own?" Jack said. Sawyer squirmed and looked at his shoes as if regretting not going with her.

"That was her idea," Zelie declared. "We were supposed to be collecting all the beans."

"Well, she must have a good reason for needing that book of spells," Jack said, changing his tone completely. He sighed. "Alright, we'll go and pick your beans. But let's do it quickly and for Pete's sake, let's not get seen. Then as soon as Ruth's out of that castle, we'll head back down to solid ground, eh?"

Max nodded vigorously. "Solid ground. I like that

part."

# CHAPTER TWENTY

## *If You Play with Fire*

A corrosive stew of anger and anxiety bubbled and fermented deep in Zelie's belly as she led the way down the side of the castle past the barn towards the beanstalk. If Max was still shrinking at all, it was happening too slowly now. There was no way of knowing what evil still lurked within him or when it might show. But Zelie seemed to be the only one with any concern that he might attack at any moment.

With its door broken off, the barn looked frozen in a breathless scream. The giant's hessian sack lay in their way and they had little choice but to weave through the mess of uprooted trees, spilled bags of grain and broken planks of wood that lay strewn over the cloud. There were even a few huge squashed pumpkins that could only have come from Jack's garden. The giant stole all of it and now, instead of feeding the villagers or sheltering the animals, it was almost useless. Zelie's fist tightened around the wand and she glared back at Max.

Attracted by the movement, the cows ambled over from the barn and Zelie slowed her pace in case Max suddenly felt another barbaric urge to eat one of them. But he showed no signs. The cows began sifting their muzzles through the jumble of supplies in search of food. When they found the opened bags of grain, they began taking turns gathering up lazy mouthfuls and chewing them while watching Zelie and the others departing. From the broken entrance of the barn came the hungry moans of other livestock who seemed to sense that there was food being eaten.

"What's in your soupcase?" Max asked, pointing to Zelie's backpack as they emerged from the shadow of the castle into the sun.

"Friends," Zelie said sharply, not bothering to correct him.

"Friends in a soupcase?" Max said, aghast. "You not be my friend, OK?"

"I don't want to be your friend," Zelie snapped. "You're the reason they're in my bag. You smashed them up with your stupid giant feet."

"Me?" Max looked confused. "Don't remember." Then after a pause, he said: "I know. Use the magic stick at them. Make it better." He was referring to the wand.

"I can't."

"OK, I try," Max said casually, plucking the wand from Zelie's hand before she could react. He held the wand up high between his thumb and forefinger and pointed it at Zelie as she thrashed to get the bag off her back and dived to get out of the way.

"Fix the friends," Max ordered.

Zelie screwed up her face as she rolled over the cloud and braced for a painful bolt of lightning and the boom of thunder. But all she could hear was the sound of a gentle breeze. Opening her eyes, she saw two glittering tunnels of light—one red and one green— streaming from the wand. The bag stood itself upright on the cloud. The zips opened and out rose the contents. Pieces of Thurin came together in the air like a self-solving jigsaw puzzle, while the flat mess of green and glue morphed into a ball that gradually took the shape of Bre. As they reformed, both gnomes appeared to be smiling. The wand let out a brief flash, sealing the cracks in Thurin and cinching Bre's yellow belt tight. The coloured tunnels disappeared and the gnomes fell to the cloud.

The effect was immediate. The three gnomes began gabbling like excited geese, not one at a time, but all at once. It was nonsense to Zelie but the gnomes seemed to understand each other, laughing and nodding every so often while they admired each other's appearance and embraced over and over.

"I didded good?" Max asked, raising his heavy eyebrows and holding out the wand. Zelie snatched it back with a scowl.

"Very good," Dresden said, in a deep voice that could have come directly from Max's mouth. "Positively excellent," he said, with exaggerated clarity. "How much wood could a woodchuck chuck. Oh what a relief."

Bre fluttered over, pushed up her hair, and introduced herself to Jack. Thurin nodded politely at each person in turn and then took to absently smoothing at his now flawless cheek with his fingertips. Max offered his apologies, which—to Zelie's irritation— the gnomes accepted as if being smashed to pieces had been only a mild bother.

"Come on," Zelie said, impatiently, as she continued on towards the beanstalk. "We're running out of time."

Sawyer seemed unafraid of Max now, and even offered to use his rope to tie up the loose folds of his clothing. The ship's sail was incredibly loose around his body now. A few times on their trip away from the castle, it had billowed out in the breeze giving Zelie a view of more of Max's skin than she cared to see. By the time Sawyer was finished with his rope, the sail fit Max's frame perfectly. Sawyer had even tailored a series of deep pouches from the excess folds of material into which, he said, Max could store the beans. Then they all climbed the beanstalk.

Max climbed like a monkey, using his oversized hands to strip the bean pods from the stem in huge bunches and piling them into the pouches Sawyer had made. He was so fast that Zelie she had not managed to collect one single pod. Jack managed to fill the various pockets of his trousers and jacket. The gnomes did not bother about the beans at all. Instead, they recounted various events of the past few days. Despite being in pieces inside a backpack, Thurin and Bre were fully aware of what had happened and Bre mimicked Madelene's voice so accurately that twice, Zelie turned the wand on her, thinking that Madelene must have teleported herself somewhere within the foliage.

The real Madelene never showed her face once. But it was due to Zelie's regular glances that she noticed Ruth appear at the front of the castle.

Ruth had the great sliding door opened just enough to fit through and she was beckoning Zelie with a furious wave of her hand. Despite Zelie's attempts to signal that there had been a change in plans, Ruth would not be moved. With a frustrated sigh, Zelie warned Sawyer to watch out for anything strange from Max and headed towards the castle.

The sun felt velvety and warm on Zelie's shoulders as she made her way across the cloud. She used to think the older villagers were strange to make such a fuss. Now, she wondered how she had lived without the sun for so long. How wonderful would the village appear if every part of it were bathed in sun? Her eyes fell on the tip of Sawyer's bottle poking from a heavy pocket in Ruth's tattered skirt. She no longer needed the water to save Jack. But now her attention was drawn to the curse and the prospect of lifting it. The words of

Sawyer's spell were fresh in her mind. She could end it right here and bring sunshine back to the land below. A flutter rose in her chest as her fingers found the remaining beans, warm and smooth, in her pocket.

Ruth was struggling under the weight of a large leather bound book attached to a heavy chain. "It's Madelene's spells. All of them," she said, as Zelie climbed the steps. "But she's chained it up and I can't open the padlock. I thought you might use your hair again, Pet."

"I can. But shouldn't we just burn it?" Zelie said. "I don't think we can carry it down with us."

"Whatever we do, we must ensure that Madelene can no longer-"

Ruth stopped mid-sentence and gave a strange shiver.

Zelie halted on the stone landing and took a step backwards as Ruth's face fell into a blank stare. Wisps of black smoke curled over her shoulders and she gave a sharp sniff as if she had been stung from behind. The smoke shot up her nose and into her ears and the spell book tipped out of her hands and fell open on the ground. Then her mouth began to curl into a cruel grimace and her shoulders stooped forwards in a familiar hunch.

Madelene appeared behind Ruth holding an empty vial. A few remaining wisps of smoke twirled within it and then vanished.

"No!" Zelie screamed, hopelessly. "Make it stop!" But it was too late.

"Insect!" screeched Ruth.

"Reverse that spell," cried Zelie and held up the wand. Her command came out in a cloud as the air turned cold in an instant. "Turn her back or I'll-"

"Uh uh uh." Madelene tutted and drew Ruth in front

of her as a human shield. "We wouldn't want an accident would we? Wands are dangerous in the hands of the ignorant."

"As if you could use it?" Zelie screamed. "You're just a selfish witch."

"And you are just an insolent little girl," snapped Madelene. "What would you know of magic?"

"I broke the curse you put on Max," spat Zelie.

"Filthy stinking oaf," shrieked Ruth.

Madelene glanced towards the beanstalk where Zelie's allies had heard Ruth cry out and were busy trying to hide.

"Indeed you seem to have shrunk my monster. But why, pray tell, did you only do half the job? And I see that damnable fool Spriggins has survived. His head must be as hard as his determination. Oh and look, how adorable. You have some little people to help you. No, not people," she laughed. "Garden gnomes! Look at them all trying to hide from me. Precious."

"I'll have that bottle," said Zelie and her hair whipped it from Ruth's pocket with a tinkle. It was heavy with water.

"Give that back, Cockroach," Ruth squealed.

"Magic hair! What fun," Madelene jeered. "I suppose you mixed a magic bean in with your shampoo did you? Ha! Did you really believe that a head of charmed hair and an assortment of incompetent fools could oppose me? You're a long way from home and way out of your league." Then she became serious. "Now put down that wand and back away before I have you shaved bald and your mouth sewn shut for your appalling acts of insubordination."

"I don't even know what that means," Zelie scoffed. She pressed the wand up against the bottle, unscrewed the lid and fumbled in her pocket for some magic beans.

Madelene's face darkened. "If you play with fire, little girl, you're going to get burnt."

"I know you're out of magic beans," Zelie said. "So I can end your curse right now and there's nothing you can do to stop me."

"Oh no," Madelene mocked, placing the back of her hand against her forehead. "She's going to cast a little spell. Are you as frightened as I am Ruth?"

"Not frightened Majesty," screeched Ruth dutifully.

"Let's see it then, little girl. Make your little spell."

Zelie put two beans in the bottle, placed her hand over the end as before. Then she chanted the words she had committed to memory. "By the power of this wand and the magic of this bean. Break this curse's bond and let nature supervene." After the flash shone through her hand, she swung the bottle in an arc, spraying its contents high into the air above the cloud. As the concoction landed, the cloud hissed and steam rose in plumes that curled off the surface and rolled up the castle steps, surrounding them.

But then Madelene began to snigger, which turned into a howling laugh that continued until the steam cleared.

Zelie's heart sank. Closest to the castle, the concoction had dissolved a jagged pit. There were a few holes where the full thickness of the cloud had evaporated and through which Zelie could see the village far below. Just beyond the holes, was a mess of clear gel that extended half the distance to the beanstalk. And beyond that, the cloud was fluffy and white and completely unaffected.

"Dear oh dear. I haven't laughed like that in years," said Madelene, breathlessly. "You silly girl. It took an elaborate curse to create that cloud. It wasn't a lucky, half-baked accident like that mildly dextrous hairstyle of yours. Did you really believe one of my spells would be that easy to reverse? I'm not even annoyed, you insignificant creature."

Zelie pointed the wand to fire it. But Madelene just smiled knowingly and grasped Ruth's shoulder, once more steering her into the path of the wand.

"Hair," Zelie said, and Madelene's eyes narrowed. "Get Ruth out of the way." A coil of golden hair shot over her shoulder. But just as quickly, Madelene opened her hand and cast out a cloud of red dust. And as soon as Zelie's hair touched it, it fell limp on the ground and retracted away from Ruth. It dragged itself over the stones and up to Zelie's shoulders like a frightened animal, losing its shine as it went. Zelie grabbed a handful of hair with her free hand. It was thin and straggly and made no sound at all.

"Hair, bring me the witch's vials... Destroy that book of spells... Tie up the witch." The orders left her lips in a desperate shriek. But nothing happened.

Madelene sniggered. "And now you know how hopeless and inferior you really are," said Madelene. "Perhaps it's not your fault that you have so little respect. I imagine you have lived your whole life under this very cloud. Much like a turtle stuck inside its own shell. How could you know my power or your duty to me as your queen? You are bereft of a servant's education. But I have decided, just now, that I will help you."

Zelie froze and the sweat rose up on her forehead. The last two times Madelene had offered help were when Ruth received a series of lightning bolts in the back and when Jack was almost killed by the giant.

"It is my duty as your queen to enrich your understanding," Madelene continued. "In fact, we have just enough time for your first lesson. Let's call this one, *the futility of resistance*."

She twisted the ring on her finger, cupped her hands to her mouth and, in that same echoing voice, began the spell to turn Max back into a giant. At first, it seemed as if Madelene's chant was having no effect: that the concoction Zelie had poured over Max might offer some sort of protection. But then to her dismay, the giant's form began to rise up from his hiding place behind the beanstalk as if he were a balloon being inflated.

Zelie shifted side to side, trying desperately to take aim at Madelene with the wand and stop her from speaking. But Madelene kept Ruth between them.

When she had finished chanting, Madelene smirked and took a firm hold on the wall while she held the other hand up high in the air and pointed to the ground. Then she lowered her arm sharply. The cloud plummeted from the sky and both Ruth and Zelie flew into the air.

As before, the cloud arrived abruptly just above the village. Zelie crumpled to the floor, winded. Shutting out the pain, she wrestled herself up on one knee while Ruth still lay splayed on the ground. And in that moment, Zelie had a clear shot at Madelene. She raised the wand.

This was her chance. If it worked, the village would be rid of Madelene. But even if it failed, she would put enough electricity through Madelene to give everybody enough time to get to safety. She tried to think selflessly. What would Beth or any of the other villagers want? In her mind she saw Madelene with her hands bound and mouth gagged behind the bars of a jail cell. But she could not free her mind of the hope that imprisoning Madelene might save her own life. The wand shook in her hand. Lightning would have to do. She aimed, careful not to point the other end at herself, and wished it to be real.

Lightning shot from each end. Zelie's aim was true and the bolt struck Madelene in the chest. But no sooner had it entered her body, than it had split into two, run up Madelene's arms, out through her fingers and straight back at Zelie, striking her to the ground.

# CHAPTER TWENTY-ONE

## *Foam and Confusion*

A blazing white light filled Zelie's vision as the lightning bolts struck her, tossing her limp body down the front stairs of the castle. Pain, like nothing she had ever felt, throbbed through every joint and muscle. Vile bitterness filled her mouth and a high-pitched hum rang in her ears until it gave way to the sound of her own body gasping for air. She felt hollow. This was the price of selfishness. Madelene must know it well, Zelie thought, though the cost was usually borne by the villagers.

Out of the haze of agony there was a distant echoing voice. She could not make out any words, just a buzzy murmur over garbled speech and the scuff of feet descending stone steps. The pain seemed to be drawing inwards to her shoulder and she could smell her own burned flesh. She blinked to clear her foggy vision. Madelene's face appeared double above her. Eager hands rummaged in her pockets and pried apart her fingers. Between slow blinks, Zelie saw the wand and her last magic bean withdraw inside Madelene's grasp.

"No," she mumbled hopelessly, and rolled her head side to side sluggishly. But this just made Madelene laugh again. A deep throaty victory laugh.

The giant's warm stench invaded Zelie's nostrils. "Fee—Fi—Fo—Fum!" he boomed. Zelie's drowsy mind brought her thoughts of Dresden. The giant's huge hunched silhouette moved across the brilliance of the sun, casting its broad shadow over Zelie's withered body. She shivered on the icy stone steps and stared blankly upwards. The giant's lips parted and a flood of sticky drool spilled into the deep gooey pits in the cloud that Zelie had made with her earlier attempt to end the curse with a hastily made concoction.

From the corner of her eye, Zelie saw the cloud peel away at Madelene's command and heard Mayor Andrews' snivelling voice as he presented the children as her 'humble servants'. Parents wailed sorrowfully as Madelene clapped her hands and warbled with evil laughter.

But then there was a chopping sound and shrieks of alarm from the villagers. Zelie willed her heavy, aching body to roll onto one elbow. Down through the hole, she saw Sawyer. He had made his way to the base of the beanstalk and had taken up the axe. To Zelie's surprise, he was swinging it with great skill. Huge chunks of beanstalk fell away with each chop. The pitch of Madelene's voice rose with concern.

"Stop it. I will not have this. By Royal order, stop, I say." When that did not work, Madelene held up the wand and commanded a shiny new golden crown for her head. The wand sparked and fired.

Some sort of instinct seemed to grip Sawyer and he held up the handle of the axe like a shield against Madelene's attack. The lightning bolt hit the shiny metal head of the axe and reflected onto the beanstalk, cleaving it from the ground with a mighty crack. Sawyer threw down the axe and ran for shelter.

The beanstalk tilted towards the castle, splintering and growling as it did. But it was so enormous that it did not fall like any normal tree. Its huge leaves were catching the wind so that it appeared to be coming down in extreme slow motion.

"Oh no, no, no," muttered Madelene, in the most distressed tone Zelie had heard from her. "No! It will not be. Not again." She opened her gown and selected an orange potion from the two vials that remained slotted into her belt. After uncorking the vial, she stooped and hastily fluttered through the pages of the leather-bound book of spells. "Where is that incantation?" she snarled.

Zelie mustered every grain of energy to get up off the ground and face her enemy. She managed only to sit.

There stooped Madelene with the wand tucked into the back of her belt—a self-serving witch hoarding the instrument of selflessness—and from somewhere deep in Zelie's mind, a thought bloomed. If Madelene had ever put a smile on someone else's face, would she have any desire to do it again? Could she ever favour a compromise over issuing a selfish command? Zelie closed her eyes. Her mind became clear and calm and her thoughts blossomed into a spell so definite in her head that she could see the words as clearly as reading them from a page. Her lips began to move.

*"The wand is the seed from which charity grows*
*And a seed needs good soil as everyone knows.*
*The witch holds the wand for no reason but greed.*
*She calls herself Queen. We must intercede.*
*So plant it within her until she is full of*
*Unselfishness, friendship, kindness and true love.*
*Treat thoughts in her mind as if they were said:*
*Good deeds be performed or lightning instead.*

*All shards must be spent, else this charm must remain.*

*The wand and the witch: make them one and the same."*

As Zelie spoke the words of the spell, the vial in Madelene's hand began to change. The orange liquid swirled until it became a bright green, casting an eerie glow on the side of Madelene's face as she swivelled around to Zelie, her mouth open and eyes wide in a mixture of horror and scorn. Frantically, she fumbled the cork into the top of the vial but the pressure inside was too great and the cork flew off with a pop. Desperation washed over Madelene's face and she shrieked, dashing the vial on the ground as she attempted to flee, all grace abandoned.

The green liquid rose up from the stone floor like a luminous ghost. A gasp escaped Madelene as the mist swept her roughly against the outer door of the castle with a wooden thump. The wand eased out of her belt and she spun around with her hands up in defence, but it was no help to her. The ghostly mist became thick and angrily dark, obscuring the wand within it. Then, with a sound like a gust of wind over a gravestone, it drew into Madelene's body.

Madelene looked windswept and swollen. She blinked as if coming out of a trance. Then she saw Zelie and her face became an inferno of molten rage. "How dare you use my own magic against me, you miserable wretch!" she screamed. "I'll destroy you." But after just one step towards Zelie, Madelene's body stiffened and shook as electricity arced between her teeth. When it stopped, she fell to her hands and knees and gave a long loud shriek filled with hate and frustration.

Zelie looked at her with bewilderment. The spell had worked. Madelene had become one with the wand. The lightning that would have otherwise shot from each end was now punishing her evil thoughts from within her body.

Zelie had no time to celebrate as Madelene shifted her furious glare to the giant. "Kill her, Monster!" she sang in a wavering electrical soprano, as another lightning bolt unleashed within her.

The giant's shadow moved across the sun. There was no escape now. Squinting at the silhouette of the giant, and behind him the falling beanstalk, Zelie knew doom was twice upon her.

But then she noticed something unusual about the outline of the giant's head against the bright sky. Her first dazed thought was that the blobs bulging from the giant's ears might be the earplugs she had made earlier. But then she saw that the blobs had feet. A tired but grateful smile tugged gently at the corners of her mouth.

"Right then Bre, when you're ready," said Jack's voice from somewhere nearby.

The feet of one of the blobs began kicking to free itself from the giant's ear canal and, as it lowered itself amongst the hairs sprouting from the giant's shoulder, it became the tiny outline of a gnome in a dress. Her little mouth moved in a whisper.

Obeying this quiet command, the giant brought down both huge fists on the front of the castle, smashing it to rubble with Madelene still inside. The last thing Zelie saw, before the stones covered the entrance, was Madelene, stiff as a board with sparks running between her teeth and her hair buzzing in a frizzy halo around her head.

Beneath the slow falling beanstalk, the giant wrestled at the flap of cloud that Madelene had peeled back to make her announcement to the Mayor. With a loud grunt, he tore it from its rubbery hinge and dragged it so that it fell through the hole.

"Time to go, Squirrel," said Jack, as his strong arms gathered her up from the castle steps. "Beg your pardon

Bre. But could you give us a hand to get down?"

At first, Zelie thought that *give us a hand* was one of those expressions she had come to accept as normal from Jack. But she was about to find out that he meant it quite literally.

In a voice that sounded exactly like Madelene, Bre issued an uncharacteristically rude command. With a grunt, the giant crouched and placed his huge hand at the base of the stone steps. The next moment, Jack was pushing Zelie onto the giant's warm palm. Ruth arrived behind her spitting ice crystals as she ran off a series of curses and threats at everyone and everything she saw. The giant lifted them up and jumped through the hole, landing silently on the slab of cloud he had thrown down earlier.

The shadow and cool moist air encircled Zelie. It felt familiar, but ill-fitting. It was like the feeling you get when you sit in a chair built for a younger child. It was once the right size, but not any more. Meanwhile, the village she should have known so well was now a foreign wasteland. From high up on the giant's hand, she could see from the cliffs all the way to the other side of the island. There was not a single house that had not either had its roof lifted from its walls or been completely swept off its foundations.

The crushed remains of the terrace houses had been cleared away and only the concrete slabs remained. On one of them, babies and children numbering about fifty had been assembled in a circle. Some were sleeping; others were calmly playing with other children or with dusty toys that must have been saved from the ruin. Meanwhile, around the circle of children, adults— either holding their reclaimed children or other items of value—were running about in random directions, mostly away from the giant, tripping over the rubble and wreckage.

A loud crack sounded from above the cloud as the beanstalk hit the castle. Bricks rained down through the hole in the cloud, narrowly missing the circle of children and waking up those who had fallen asleep. The cloud began to sag under the combined weight of the beanstalk and the castle. The children pointed and cooed and laughed and clapped, oblivious to the danger. The parents, like ants at the first splash of rain, scrambled over each other for cover at double speed. By strange contrast, Sawyer emerged from the mayhem, emboldened after his part in felling the beanstalk, with a look of calm determination. It was not over yet. The cloud continued to sag, pressing down on the giant and forcing him into a stoop.

"Kids!" Zelie shouted, her strength restored. "Who wants a ride on a giant?"

Like her, the children had grown up not knowing the dangers of the world and so the ones who could understand began a chorus of 'me, me, me' while the babies gazed at her blankly. Sawyer gave a nod of understanding and began to gather up the smaller children in his arms.

On Bre's command, the giant lowered both hands either side of the circle of children and in less than twenty seconds, Jack, Sawyer, Zelie and the gnomes had ushered, carried, chased or—in the case of the gnomes—been chased onto one of the giant's two hands. Grunting under the weight of the castle-laden cloud, the giant squeezed his way free, obliterating the fallen panels of the twisted fence as he went. He clomped down the hill and over the rubble strewn about the park, but he did not stop there. On Bre's command, he turned and waded into the sea until he was waist-deep in front of the cliffs. For some inexplicable reason, the entire ocean gave off a long charge of light, like a prolonged flash.

The giant turned back towards the land, giving his passengers one final glimpse of the intact cloud before it split like a shopping bag filled with too heavy a load. The castle's remains burst through. Bricks and broken beams thumped onto the ground and splashed into the shallow water near the shore.

A moment later, the underside of the cloud dipped and rippled as the rest of the beanstalk landed on it full-length, causing a howling gust of wind that was as violent as it was brief. Then all was silent. Even Jack was speechless; his mouth was pressed into a line. Zelie knew why. They had defeated the witch but somehow it did not feel like a victory. The village was destroyed and now the cloud hovered so low that Zelie felt tight in the chest just looking at it. She was reminded of the ever-shrinking worm tunnel. But this felt worse. At least she could escape the tunnel.

Sawyer gave her an asymmetric smile until Ruth shattered the peace with a rude name and told him to brush his filthy teeth before showing them in public. Some of the nearby children started crying, which Zelie assumed was because of Ruth's voice or the intense cold. Then one of the older children pulled on Sawyer's sleeve.

"My eyes hurt," she said. "What was that bright light?"

"I don't know," Sawyer said.

But Zelie did. It was suddenly clear. Before Max became a giant again, he had almost all of the magic beans in the pockets that Sawyer had made for him. When the giant waded out into the sea water, they must have dissolved the way that first bean did in the hair basin. The whole ocean had become a concoction. But what was anyone to do with it? She wondered if it might make the giant's legs even more powerful or give special powers to the dark hairs that sprouted from them. Both possibilities seemed equally ridiculous. The giant was wading towards shore now and kicking aside the castle remains as easily as if they were made of Lego.

The ridge of cloud was sagging under the weight of the beanstalk above, blocking the way back to shore. The only way to get under it was to get into the freezing water and swim—which none of them knew how to do. But the giant would not be stopped. Bre's instructions seemed to be as compelling as Madelene's and the giant had been told to get to dry land. He butted the ridge with his head and—to Zelie's surprise—it shifted, as the entire beanstalk hopped ever so slightly towards shore. The giant seemed encouraged by this result. Churning up the sea water as he went, he charged at the ridge of cloud and rammed it like an angry bull, sending the beanstalk bouncing and rolling right over to the other side of the island.

Now Zelie could see sunlight shining through the gash where the castle had fallen through, but she still felt the weight of sadness. The rest of the land still shivered under the cold thick sheet of cloud that now hung so low. She sighed at the thought of the children crowding under an ugly gash in the cloud for glimpse of beauty. She wanted them to witness all the colours of dawn as she had done. They should be allowed to see the sparkle of stars across the entire night sky. She wanted the older generation to feel the warmth of the sun every day and put an end to their yearning. She wanted the village to regain the life they all said it used to have. Sitting on the palm of a giant, surrounded by children and friends and in the midst of ruin, she felt a strange contentment, a connection with the island and its people and even the giant: as if they were all one living, breathing, pulsing being. If only she could lift it up, give it wings, set it free and watch it soar. There was nothing she wanted more. In that moment she knew— without a shred of doubt—that she could end the curse. If only she still had the wand.

Once the giant reached the shore, he kicked away the scattered debris until he had cleared a space. Some of the parents began to emerge cautiously from behind upside down cars, piles of rubble, and sheets of metal that were crumpled so severely that they looked like they belonged on a large accordion. They looked up at the giant with a mixture of hope and fear in their eyes. The giant had just bent forward to set down his passengers when, suddenly, inside the submerged remains of the castle, electricity crackled and sparks danced. The giant straightened and gave a grunt of resignation.

Whether she was protected by some sort of magic charm or through sheer luck, Madelene had survived. Gasps rose up from the parents on the ground. Zelie shrieked, but not with fear. If the whole ocean was a concoction and the witch and wand were still bound together, surely she could use their combined power. Desperate words spluttered from her mouth.

"By the power of this wand and the magic of this bean. Break this curse's bond and let nature supervene."

As Zelie finished her spell, there was a deep rumbling that sounded as if it was coming from the very core of the earth. The sea water amidst the castle stones began to froth violently. It churned and roiled outwards across the sea, spitting white foam onto the shore and up over the land. The rumbling grew louder and the frothing more intense. Zelie was more frightened than

199

ever. Had she been too hasty in casting her spell?

Up, up, up towards the cloud the foam rose, like milk boiling on a stove. In a few moments, it had risen above the giant's hands and up to Zelie's chest. In a panic, she closed her eyes and inhaled as deeply as her lungs would allow. As the foam engulfed her completely, she wondered fearfully if she had just taken her last breath. The playful giggle of nearby children told her that the foam was safe to breathe and when she did, the air tasted clean and pure. Though, when she opened her eyes, she could see nothing but tiny bubbles.

Her shoes touched down on the ground and it was only then that she realised the giant's hand was gone from beneath her. The foam had taken her weight and carried her down. Her hands found the soft mossy cover of the shoreline.

The roar of the storm began to subside and the bubbles in the foam began to pop in front of her eyes until it was so thin that she could make out Ruth's unclenched face, smiling.

"It's working," Zelie gasped.

The giant seemed to have disappeared altogether and the children whooped playfully on the shoreline, diving over one another to catch the last clumps of foam as they dissolved. A teenage boy that Zelie had never seen before was dipping and diving among them. She was relieved to see Jack, Sawyer and even the gnomes were all unharmed. A discontented growl came from the cloud. Zelie flinched at first, expecting some new threat. But then she saw that the cloud was dissolving. It shrivelled like thin plastic over a flame, its last grey wisps unable to hold up the beanstalk which tore through and splashed into the ocean on the far side of the island.

Beams of warm sunlight shone down to the rapturous shrieks of the children as it warmed their pale skin for the first time. The parents cooed with unrestrained awe. Zelie marvelled at the bright blue of the ocean and the various vibrant shades of colour the sun had revealed in the mossy shore and the ocean beyond and she found herself laughing with surprised delight. She wrapped Sawyer up in a hug so tight it made him squeak. The gnomes pattered over, latched onto her legs and began to sing a merry tune that Zelie wished she knew so she could sing along.

Meanwhile, Jack approached the teenager who had been playing with the kids and tapped him on the shoulder, laughing. The boy turned. And when he saw Jack, he jumped up and down excitedly like a child after too much chocolate. They embraced and huge tears began flowing down Jack's cheeks as he beat the boy on the back and ruffled his hair. This was no teenager but a child whose body did not match his young mind. This was Max as he should have been if Madelene had not stolen his youth and made him a giant. His curse had ended too. Zelie beamed.

The parents began to stream into the park, holding and kissing their children and acknowledging the blue sky with obliging smiles as the children pointed. But they seemed so relieved at having their children safe that they might have responded the same way if it were hailing.

Mayor Andrews appeared in front of Zelie, fingers laced and sparkling smile switched on, though his suit was in tatters. Somehow he had already heard how she had ended the curse. A worried shiver ran up Zelie's spine at the thought of punishment. But she had no need to worry. The Mayor seemed unconcerned with laws. He gushed praise and admiration while he shook her hand so hard she thought her arm might come off. He even invited her to call him Douglas. Perhaps, at long last, he had changed his opinions on magic.

As the Mayor disappeared to find other hands to shake, Beth appeared. She hugged Zelie and stroked her hair, not seeming to mind that it had returned to its straggly state. Zelie smiled so hard that her cheeks ached.

There was a single shriek from the water's edge which—at first—Zelie took to be a parent's delight. But then there was an eruption of horrified gasps from the crowd. Beth's smile dropped away and she thrust Zelie behind her. With a squeal Sawyer, squatted behind the gnomes. Then he stood up as if to correct himself, and puffed out his chest in a way that looked more uneasy and foolish than brave. Ignoring Mayor Andrew's attempts to calm them, parents swept their children into their arms and fled from the shore in mass retreat. Then Zelie saw why.

Sopping wet and with a face like thunder, Madelene waded out of the water onto the shore. Her fierce eyes scanned left and right until her gaze met Zelie's. Madelene stopped and her whole body shook with rage. Her face twisted into a scowl as she reached inside her gown for her very last magic vial. At the same time, Beth withdrew the polkadot bottle from the pocket of her coat. But before Beth could cast a defensive spell, Madelene gave a yell and her body went tense. Electricity looped and danced all over her wet clothes and hair and the glass vial shattered in her tightened grip.

Madelene gave a frustrated scream as she crouched down and clawed the broken glass with her fingers. It was futile. The potion had soaked into the ground. She shot an acidic glare at Zelie causing another lightning bolt to seize her body in a painful spasm. Then she screwed her eyes tightly closed, as if to prevent any further thoughts of revenge, and hurried away through the park.

When Madelene had disappeared through the rubble and out of view, Jack spun around, smirked at Zelie and put an arm around Max.

"That's the finest magic I've ever seen, Squirrel. You'd have made your father proud."

# CHAPTER TWENTY-TWO
## *A New Dawn*

It took many weeks for the village to be cleared of rubble and months for all the houses to be rebuilt, but nobody ever complained. The villagers sang songs as they worked together with their arms and legs bare to the gentle warmth of the sun. As the months went by, their pale skin became darker and healthier but their smiles remained broad. Zelie helped in the mornings but lost interest by lunchtime. To her relief, nobody begrudged her disappearing in the afternoons to play with her friends or finding somewhere to explore or to bathe in the sun.

Zelie's curse-ending actions became something of a legend around the village. Zelie Sunshine, they called her. To her mild unease, she was greeted with applause wherever she went. Sawyer, on the other hand, came to love the attention. When people gave a cheer, he bowed in all directions, shook hands with the men, blew kisses to the ladies, and gave high fives to the children. He even accepted invitations to make speeches at business conferences. He took the gnomes along to them, partly because they loved telling the story and partly so Sawyer did not have to. He had hundreds of cardboard axes printed up so he could hand them out at the end of each conference and pose for photographs with the people who attended. Sawyer said the axes were supposed to be a metaphor: something about taking action instead of accepting defeat. It sounded like nonsense to Zelie but she was happy for him. He had found a tiny magic bean of bravery within himself and it had grown into a great towering beanstalk of courage. In a way, Zelie felt as proud about helping Sawyer as she did about her part in ending the curse.

Occasionally, people would report having seen Madelene coming and going from a cave on the far north coast of the island. She had managed to put a stop to the electrical shocks by living a simple life, catching fish from the sea and eating root vegetables and berries from the forest. Madelene had been so horrible to the villagers, but all the same, Zelie hoped that one day she might make enough selfless spells to deplete the wand's power and rid herself of the charm.

Mayor Andrews abolished the laws preventing magic and very soon afterwards, Jack happened to find some magic beans. In truth, something must be lost in order to be found. Zelie knew what the villagers all suspected: that Jack really had the beans all along. He never did empty his pockets after the harvest at the top of the beanstalk.

Max became an apprentice of sorts to Jack and the two were rarely apart, always with matching smiles and often making jokes and laughing. At one time or another, they must have helped every single person in the village with some aspect of fixing up their houses or re-growing their gardens which were, more often than not, planted out with charmed seeds. Zelie's favourite was the tree they planted in Mayor Andrew's garden. Instead of fruit, it grew lumps of chocolate the size of ping pong balls with variously flavoured fillings. Zelie had tried every flavour but caramel. They were the ones Ruth liked best and Sawyer always picked them all for her before Zelie ever had a chance.

Soon after the chocolate tree incident, the Mayor put—what he called—'a regulatory certification' on magic. He made it a requirement to complete a course called 'The Responsible Use of Magic' and to carry a special licence before a person could cast a spell legally. Ruth was appointed as the instructor for the course and Zelie was first in the village to get a licence. Max was the second.

Jack refused to take the course and, while Max and Zelie attended, he coaxed Beth into helping him to create some sort of super-charmed seeds. From them, he grew a vine which fruited pumpkins the size of small houses. Mayor Andrews was not pleased, particularly because it was planted next to the chocolate tree in his own garden. But to avoid the embarrassment of such a well-respected citizen performing uncertified magic, he granted Jack an honorary magic licence for his services to the villagers and Jack agreed not to plant any more charmed seeds in the Mayor's garden.

It was over a month before the water in the ocean warmed up. Soon, swimming was the villagers' favourite weekend activity and many of the children spent afternoons taking turns to jump into the water from a pier that was built from the remains of the castle. Zelie preferred the other side of the island where the fallen beanstalk provided an enormous floating pontoon on which to bask in the sun.

One day, Beth sat Zelie down and—after soaking a great number of tissues—told her what had happened to her father. When the tissues ran out, her tears dripped on the table and in her tea as she recounted how Zelie's father had stood up to Madelene at the base of the beanstalk and how, in reply, Madelene had put a dark charm on his legs that caused him to march out into the ocean and drown. It was not long before Beth was smiling again as she recalled the many happy memories. Zelie particularly liked hearing how, as a baby, she would climb up on his shoulders and pull his ears this way and that to steer him around the village. Apparently, she would laugh at him when he pulled funny faces, but nothing made her giggle and clap more than when he winked one eye at her. She wished she could remember that.

At Christmas, Jack and Max made pumpkin soup for the entire island. The celebration was held in the park where Mayor Andrews agreed to allow Zelie to plant one of Jack's magic beans. The beanstalk sang its lovely tune and grew to its full height in just three days. From then on, it provided all the beans the villagers needed for their spells. A flower garden was set out around the new beanstalk and named in memory of Zelie's father.

On clear nights, Zelie would climb as far as she could up the beanstalk. Occasionally, Sawyer and the gnomes would go with her. Max always refused, preferring to keep his feet on solid ground. After ten years living on the cloud, Zelie could understand why. Without her magic hair, she could never climb more than half way to the top. But from high above the village, Zelie would lay on a leaf and gaze up at the night sky. There was one star that seemed to catch her eye every time. Every so often it would wink at her and she would smile.

Every day, Zelie looked up at the sky with gratitude. Even on days that were overcast, the cloud always moved and changed. It was never as dull as it had been with the curse. Sometimes she thought she saw a giant in the clouds, and sometimes a wand or a castle. And during storms, she would watch through her bedroom window as lightning cut bright jagged lines through the dark. She would gasp and smile when a bolt struck close by and the thunder made the entire house rumble. For some reason, these things stirred up a longing inside her. Secretly, she yearned for a new challenge and the thrill of rising above it. Perhaps one day she would have the chance to go on another great adventure. One day soon, she hoped.

# Acknowledgements

Firstly and most importantly, I want to thank you—the reader. If it wasn't for you buying this book (or borrowing it from the library), I might be forced to find a far less interesting job. Thank you also for your reviews on Amazon and Goodreads which encourage others to choose one of my books to read next. I hope to entertain you with refined versions of the stories that rattle around constantly inside my brain and will surely pour out my ears if I don't get them on paper first.

The rest of the people I want to thank know who they are. I can't express how much I appreciate their help and support and if I tried, I would surely cause other readers to feel quite nauseated. But there is one person for whom I will risk the mildest of queasiness among readers, and that's my daughter, Ember. She was the one who encouraged me to write in the first place and whose overwhelming favouritism among authors kept me going through the many drafts and edits of this story.